HUNTERS OF THE DUSK

THE SAGA OF DARREN SHAN
BOOK 7

Other titles by
DARREN SHAN

THE SAGA OF DARREN SHAN

THE DEMONATA

*Also available on audio

DARREN SHAN

HUNTERS OF THE DUSK

THE SAGA OF DARREN SHAN
BOOK 7

HarperCollins *Children's Books*

Hunt for Darren Shan
on the web at
www.darrenshan.com

First published in Great Britain by HarperCollins *Children's Books* 2002
This edition published 2009
HarperCollins *Children's Books* is a division of HarperCollins*Publishers* Ltd,
1 London Bridge Street
London SE1 9GF

The HarperCollins website address is:
www.harpercollins.co.uk

5

Text copyright © 2001 Darren Shan

ISBN-13 978 0 00 793899 5

The author asserts the moral right to
be identified as the author of the work.

Printed and bound by
CPI Group (UK) Ltd, Croydon, CR0 4YY

Mixed Sources
Product group from well-managed
forests and other controlled sources
www.fsc.org Cert no. SW-COC-1806
© 1996 Forest Stewardship Council

FSC is a non-profit international organisation established to promote the
responsible management of the world's forests. Products carrying the FSC
label are independently certified to assure consumers that they come
from forests that are managed to meet the social, economic and
ecological needs of present and future generations.

Find out more about HarperCollins and the environment at
www.harpercollins.co.uk/green

For:

Shirley & Derek – "Beauty and the Beast"

Sparring partners:
Gillie Russell & Zoë Clarke

Ringside crew:
The Christopher Little clan

OBEs (Order of the Bloody Entrails) to:
Kerri "carve yer guts up" Goddard-Kinch
"la femme fatale" Christine Colinet

PROLOGUE

IT WAS an age of tragic mistakes. For me, the tragedy began fourteen years earlier when, mesmerized by a vampire's amazing performing tarantula, I stole it from him. After an initially successful theft, everything went to hell, and I paid for my crime with my humanity. Faking my own death, I left my family and home, and travelled the world with the Cirque Du Freak, as the assistant to a blood-drinking creature of the night.

My name's Darren Shan. I'm a half-vampire.

I'm also – through a series of events so astounding I still have trouble believing they really happened – a Vampire Prince. The Princes are the leaders of the vampire clan, respected and obeyed by all. There are only five of them — the others are Paris Skyle, Mika Ver Leth, Arrow and Vancha March.

I'd been a Prince for six years, living within the Halls of Vampire Mountain (the stronghold of the clan), learning the customs and traditions of my people, and how to be a vampire of good standing. I'd also been learning the ways of warfare, and how to use weapons. The rules of battle were essential components of any vampire's education, but now more so than ever — because we were at war.

Our opponents were the vampaneze, our purple-skinned blood-cousins. They're a lot like vampires in many ways, but alien to us in one key area — they kill whenever they drink blood. Vampires don't harm those they feed from — we simply take a small amount of blood from each human we target — but vampaneze believe it's shameful to feed without draining their victims dry.

Though there was no love lost between the vampires and vampaneze, for hundreds of years an uneasy truce had existed between the two clans. That changed six years ago when a group of vampaneze — aided by a vampire traitor called Kurda Smahlt — stormed Vampire Mountain in an attempt to seize control of the Hall of Princes. We defeated them (thanks largely to my discovery of the plot prior to their assault), then interrogated the survivors, baffled by why they should choose to attack.

Unlike vampires, vampaneze had no leaders — they were entirely democratic — but when they split from the vampires six hundred years ago, a mysterious, powerful magician known as Mr Tiny paid them a visit and placed the Coffin of Fire in their possession. This coffin burnt alive anyone who lay within it — but Mr Tiny said that one night a man would lie down in it and step out unharmed, and that man would lead them into a victorious war with the vampires, establishing the vampaneze as the unopposed rulers of the night.

During the interrogation, we learnt to our horror that the Lord of the Vampaneze had finally arisen, and vampaneze across the world were preparing for the violent, bloody war to come.

Once our assailants had been put to a painful death, word spread from Vampire Mountain like wildfire: "We're at war with the vampaneze!" And we'd been locked in combat with them ever since, fighting grimly, desperate to disprove Mr Tiny's dark prophecy — that we were destined to lose the war and be wiped from the face of the earth...

CHAPTER ONE

IT WAS another long, tiring night in the Hall of Princes. A Vampire General called Staffen Irve was reporting to me and Paris Skyle. Paris was the oldest living vampire, with more than eight hundred years under his belt. He had flowing white hair, a long, grey beard, and had lost his right ear in a fight many decades ago.

Staffen Irve had been active in the field for three years, and had been giving us a quick rundown of his experiences in the War of the Scars, as it had come to be known (a reference to the scars on our fingertips, the common mark of a vampire or vampaneze). It was a strange war. There were no big battles and neither side used missile-firing weapons — vampires and vampaneze fight only with hand to hand weapons like swords, clubs and spears. The war was a series of isolated skirmishes, three or four vampires at a time pitting themselves against a similar number of vampaneze, fighting to the death.

"There was four of us 'gainst three of them," Staffen Irve said, telling us about one of his more recent encounters. "But my lads was dry behind the tonsils, while the vampaneze was battle-hardy. I killed one of 'em but the others got away, leaving two of my lads dead and the third with a useless arm."

"Have any of the vampaneze spoken of their Lord?" Paris asked.

"No, Sire. Those I take alive only laugh at my questions, even under torture."

In the six years that we'd been hunting for their Lord, there'd been no sign of him. We knew he hadn't been blooded – various vampaneze had told us that he was learning their ways before becoming one of them – and the general opinion was that if we were to have any chance of thwarting Mr Tiny's predictions, we had to find and kill their Lord before he assumed full control of the clan.

A cluster of Generals was waiting to speak with Paris. They moved forward as Staffen Irve departed, but I signalled them back. Picking up a mug of warm blood, I passed it to the one-eared Prince. He smiled and drank deeply, then wiped red stains from around his mouth with the back of a trembling hand — the responsibility of running the war council was taking its toll on the ancient vampire.

"Do you want to call it a night?" I asked, worried about Paris's health.

He shook his head. "The night is young," he muttered.

"But you are not," said a familiar voice behind me — Mr Crepsley. The vampire in the red cloak spent most of his time by my side, advising and encouraging me. He was in a peculiar position. As an ordinary vampire, he held no recognizable rank, and could be commanded by the lowliest of Generals. Yet as my guardian he wielded the unofficial powers of a Prince (since I followed his advice practically all the time). The reality was that Mr Crepsley was second in charge only to Paris Skyle, yet nobody openly acknowledged this. Vampire protocol — go figure!

"You should rest," Mr Crepsley said to Paris, laying a hand on the Prince's shoulder. "This war will run a long time. You must not exhaust yourself too early. We will have need of you later."

"Rot!" Paris laughed. "You and Darren are the future. I am the past, Larten. I will not live to see the end of this war if it drags on as long as we fear. If I do not make my mark now, I never will."

Mr Crepsley started to object, but Paris silenced him with the crooking of a finger. "An old owl hates to be told how young and virile he is. I am on my last legs, and anyone who says otherwise is a fool, a liar, or both."

Mr Crepsley tilted his head obediently. "Very well. I will not argue with you."

"I should hope not," Paris sniffed, then shifted tiredly on his throne. "But this *has* been a taxing night. I will talk with these Generals, then crawl off to my coffin to sleep. Will Darren be able to manage without me?"

"Darren will manage," Mr Crepsley said confidently, and stood slightly behind me as the Generals advanced, ready to advise when required.

Paris didn't make his coffin by dawn. The Generals had much to argue about – by studying reports on the movements of the vampaneze they were trying to pinpoint the possible hiding place of their Lord – and it was close to midday before the ancient Prince slipped away.

I treated myself to a short break, grabbed some food, then heard from three of the Mountain's fighting tutors, who were training the latest batch of Generals. After that I had to send two new Generals out into the field for their first taste of combat. I quickly went through the small ceremony – I had to daub their foreheads with vampire blood and mutter an ancient war prayer over them – then wished them luck and sent them off to kill vampaneze — or die.

Then it was time for vampires to approach me with a wide range of problems and queries. As a Prince I was expected to deal with every sort of subject under the moon. I was only a young, inexperienced half-vampire, who'd become a Prince more by default than merit, but the members of the clan placed their trust completely in their Princes, and I was afforded the same degree of respect as Paris or any of the others.

When the last vampire had departed, I snatched about three hours of sleep, in a hammock which I'd strung up at the rear of the Hall. When I woke, I ate some half-cooked, salted boar meat, washed down with water and followed by a small mug of blood. Then it was back to my throne for more planning, plotting and reports.

CHAPTER TWO

I SNAPPED out of sleep to the sound of screaming.

Jerking awake, I fell out of my hammock, on to the hard, cold floor of my rocky cell. My hand automatically darted for the short sword which I kept strapped by my side at all times. Then the fog of sleep cleared and I realized it was only Harkat, having a nightmare.

Harkat Mulds was a Little Person, a short creature who wore blue robes and worked for Mr Tiny. He'd been human once, though he didn't remember who he used to be, or when or where he lived. When he died, his soul remained trapped on Earth, until Mr Tiny brought him back to life in a new, stunted body.

"Harkat," I mumbled, shaking him roughly. "Wake up. You're dreaming again."

Harkat had no eyelids, but his large green eyes dimmed when he was asleep. Now the light in them flared and he moaned loudly, rolling out of his hammock, as I had moments before. "Dragons!" he screamed, voice muffled by the mask he always wore — he wasn't able to breathe normal air for more than ten or twelve hours, and without the mask he'd die. "Dragons!"

"No," I sighed. "You've been dreaming."

Harkat stared at me with his unnatural green eyes, then relaxed and tugged his mask down, revealing a wide, grey, jagged gash of a mouth. "Sorry, Darren. Did I wake ... you?"

"No," I lied. "I was up already."

I swung back on to my hammock and sat gazing at Harkat. There was no denying he was an ugly build of a creature. Short and squat, with dead, grey skin, no visible ears or a nose — he had ears stitched beneath the skin of his scalp, but was without a sense of smell or taste. He'd no hair, round, green eyes, sharp little teeth and a dark grey tongue. His face had been stitched together, like Frankenstein's monster.

Of course, I was no model myself — few vampires were! My face, body and limbs were laced with scars and burn marks, many picked up during my Trials of Initiation (which I'd passed at my second attempt, two years ago). I was also as bald as a baby, as a result of my first set of Trials, when I'd been badly burnt.

Harkat was one of my closest friends. He'd saved my life twice, when I was attacked by a wild bear on the trail to Vampire Mountain, then in a fight with savage boars during my first, failed Trials of Initiation. It bothered me to see him so disturbed by the nightmares which had been plaguing him for the last few years.

"Was this nightmare the same as the others?" I asked.

"Yes," he nodded. "I was wandering in a vast wasteland. The sky was red. I was searching for something but I didn't ... know what. There were pits full of stakes. A dragon attacked. I fought it off but ... another appeared. Then another. Then..." He sighed miserably.

Harkat's speech had improved greatly since he'd first started speaking. In the beginning he'd had to pause for breath after every two or three words, but he'd learnt to control his breathing technique and now only stalled during long sentences.

"Were the shadow men there?" I asked. Sometimes he dreamt of shadowy figures who chased and tormented him.

"Not this time," he said, "though I think they'd have appeared if you ... hadn't woken me up." Harkat was sweating — his sweat was a pale green colour — and his shoulders shook slightly. He suffered greatly in his sleep, and stayed awake as long as he could, only sleeping four or five hours out of every seventy-two.

"Want something to eat or drink?" I asked.

"No," he said. "Not hungry." He stood and stretched his burly arms. He was only wearing a cloth around his waist, so I could see his smooth stomach and chest — Harkat had no nipples or belly button.

"It's good to see you," he said, pulling on his blue robes, which he'd never grown out of the habit of wearing. "It's been ages since ... we got together."

"I know," I groaned. "This war business is killing me, but I can't leave Paris to deal with it alone. He needs me."

"How is Sire Skyle?" Harkat asked.

"Bearing up. But it's hard. So many decisions to make, so many troops to organize, so many vampires to send to their death."

We were silent a while, thinking about the War of the Scars and the vampires – including some very good friends of ours – who'd perished in it.

"How've you been?" I asked Harkat, shrugging off the morbid thoughts.

"Busy," he said. "Seba's working me harder all the time." After a few months of milling around Vampire Mountain, Harkat had gone to work for the quartermaster – Seba Nile – who was in charge of stocking and maintaining the Mountain's stores of food, clothes and weapons. Harkat started out moving crates and sacks around, but he'd learnt quickly about supplies and how to keep up with the needs of the vampires, and now served as Seba's senior assistant.

"Do you have to return to the Hall of Princes soon?" Harkat asked. "Seba would like to see you. He wants to show you … some spiders." The mountain was home to thousands of arachnids, known as Ba'Halen's spiders.

"I have to go back," I said regretfully, "but I'll try to drop by soon."

"Do," Harkat said seriously. "You look exhausted. Paris is not the only one who … needs rest."

Harkat had to leave shortly afterwards to prepare for the arrival of a group of Generals. I lay in my hammock and stared at the dark rock ceiling, unable to get back to sleep. This was the cell Harkat and me had first shared when we came to Vampire Mountain. I liked this tiny cubbyhole – it was the closest thing I had to a bedroom – but rarely got to see much of it. Most of my nights were spent in the Hall of Princes, and the few free hours I had by day were normally passed eating or exercising.

I ran a hand over my bald head while I was resting and thought back over my Trials of Initiation. I'd sailed through them the second time. I didn't have to take them – as a Prince, I was under no obligation – but I wouldn't have felt right if I hadn't. By passing the Trials, I'd proved myself worthy of being a vampire.

Apart from the scars and burns, I hadn't changed much in the last six years. As a half-vampire, I only aged one year for every five that passed. I was a bit taller than when I left the Cirque Du Freak with Mr Crepsley, and my features had thickened and matured slightly. But I wasn't a full-vampire and wouldn't change vastly until I became one. As a full-vampire I'd be much stronger. I'd also be able to heal cuts with my spit, breathe out a gas which could knock people unconscious, and communicate telepathically with other vampires. Plus I'd be able to flit, which is a super-fast speed vampires can attain. On the down side, I'd be vulnerable to sunlight and couldn't move about during the day.

But all that lay far ahead. Mr Crepsley hadn't said anything about when I'd be fully blooded, but I gathered it wouldn't happen until I was an adult. That was ten or fifteen years away — my body was still that of a teenager — so I had loads of time to enjoy (or endure) my extended childhood.

I lay relaxing for another half hour, then got up and dressed. I'd taken to wearing light blue clothes, trousers and a tunic, covered by a long, regal-looking robe. My right thumb snagged on the arm of the tunic as I was pulling it on, as it often did — I'd broken the thumb six years ago and it still stuck out at an awkward angle.

Taking care not to rip the fabric on my extra tough nails — which could gouge holes in soft rock — I freed my thumb and finished dressing. I pulled on a pair of light shoes and ran a hand over my head to make sure I hadn't been bitten by ticks. They'd popped up all over the mountain recently, annoying everyone. Then I made my way back to the Hall of Princes for another long night of tactics and debate.

CHAPTER THREE

THE DOORS to the Hall of Princes could only be opened by a Prince, by laying a hand on the doors or touching a panel on the thrones inside the Hall. Nothing could breach the walls of the Hall, which had been built by Mr Tiny and his Little People centuries before.

The Stone of Blood was housed in the Hall, and was of vital importance. It was a magical artefact. Any vampire who came to the mountain (most of the three thousand vampires in the world had made the trek at least once) laid their hands on the Stone and let it absorb some of their blood. The Stone could then be used to track that vampire down. So, if Mr Crepsley wanted to know where Arrow was, he had only to lay his hands on the Stone and think about him, and within seconds he'd have a fix on the Prince. Or, if he thought of an area, the Stone would tell him how many vampires were there.

I couldn't use the Stone of Blood to search for others — only full-vampires were able to do that — but I could be traced through it, since it had taken blood from me when I became a Prince.

If the Stone ever fell into the hands of the vampaneze, they could use it to track down all the vampires who'd bonded with it. Hiding from them would be impossible. They'd annihilate us. Because of this danger, some vampires wanted to destroy the Stone of Blood — but there was a legend that it could save us in our hour of greatest need.

I was thinking about all this while Paris used the Stone of Blood to manoeuvre troops in the field. As reports reached us of vampaneze positions, Paris used the Stone to check where his Generals were, then communicated telepathically with them, giving them orders to move from place to place. It was this which drained him so deeply. Others could have used the Stone, but as a Prince, Paris's word was law, and it was quicker for him to deliver the orders himself.

While Paris focused on the Stone, Mr Crepsley and me spent much of our time putting field reports together and building up a clear picture of the movements of the vampaneze. Many other Generals were also doing this, but it was our job to take their findings, sort through them, pick out the more important nuggets, and make suggestions to Paris. We had loads of maps, with pins stuck in to mark the positions of vampires and vampaneze.

Mr Crepsley had been intently studying a map for ten minutes, and he looked worried. "Have you seen this?" he asked eventually, summoning me over.

I stared at the map. There were three yellow flags and two red flags stuck close together around a city. We used five main colours to keep track of things. Blue flags for vampires. Yellow for vampaneze. Green for vampaneze strongholds — cities and towns which they defended like bases. White flags were stuck in places where we'd won fights. Red flags where we'd lost.

"What am I looking for?" I asked, staring at the yellow and red flags. My eyes were bleary from lack of sleep and too much concentrating on maps and poorly scrawled reports.

"The name of the city," Mr Crepsley said, running a fingernail over it.

The name meant nothing to me at first. Then my head cleared. "That's your original home," I muttered. It was the city where Mr Crepsley had lived when he was human. Twelve years ago, he'd returned, taking me and Evra Von — a snake-boy from the Cirque Du Freak — with him, to stop a mad vampaneze called Murlough, who'd gone on a killing spree.

"Find the reports," Mr Crepsley said. There was a number on each flag, linking it to reports in our files, so we knew exactly what each flag represented. After a few minutes, I found the relevant sheets of paper and quickly scanned them.

"Of the vampaneze seen there," I muttered, "two were heading into the city. The other was leaving. The first red flag's from a year ago — four Generals were killed in a large clash with several vampaneze."

"And the second red flag marks the spot where Staffen Irve lost two of his men," Mr Crepsley said. "It was when I was adding this flag to the map that I noticed the degree of activity around the city."

"Do you think it means anything?" I asked. It was unusual for so many vampaneze to be sighted in one location.

"I am not sure," he said. "The vampaneze may have made a base there, but I do not see why — it is out of the way of their other strongholds."

"We could send someone to check," I suggested.

He considered that, then shook his head. "We have already lost too many Generals there. It is not a strategically important site. Best to leave it alone."

Mr Crepsley rubbed the long scar which divided the flesh on the left side of his face and went on staring at the map. He'd cut his orange crop of hair tighter than usual — most vampires were cutting their hair short, because of the ticks — and he looked almost bald in the strong light of the Hall.

"It bothers you, doesn't it?" I noted.

He nodded. "If they *have* set up a base, they must be feeding on the humans. I still consider it home, and I do not like to think of my spiritual neighbours and relations suffering at the hands of the vampaneze."

"We could send in a team to flush them out."

He sighed. "That would not be fitting. I would be putting personal considerations before the welfare of the clan. If I ever get out in the field, I shall check on the situation myself, but there is no need to send others."

"What are the odds on you and me ever getting out of here?" I asked wryly. I didn't enjoy fighting, but after six years cooped up inside the mountain, I'd have given my fingernails for a few nights out in the open, even if it meant taking on a dozen vampaneze single-handed.

"The way things stand — poor," Mr Crepsley admitted. "I think we will be stuck here until the end of the war. If one of the other Princes suffers a serious injury and withdraws from battle, we might have to replace him. Otherwise..." He drummed his fingers on the map and grimaced.

"*You* don't have to stay," I said quietly. "There are plenty of others who could guide me."

He barked a laugh. "There are plenty who would steer you," he agreed, "but how many would clip you around the ear if you made an error?"

"Not many," I chuckled.

"They think of you as a Prince," he said, "whereas I still think of you first and foremost as a meddlesome little brat with a *penchant* for stealing spiders."

"Charming!" I huffed. I knew he was kidding – Mr Crepsley always treated me with the respect my position deserved – but there was some truth to his teasing. There was a special bond between Mr Crepsley and me, like between a father and son. He could say things to me that no other vampire would dare. I'd be lost without him.

Placing the map of Mr Crepsley's former home to one side, we returned to the more important business of the night, little dreaming of the events which would eventually lead us back to the city of Mr Crepsley's youth, or the awful confrontation with evil that awaited us there.

CHAPTER FOUR

THE HALLS and tunnels of Vampire Mountain were buzzing with excitement — Mika Ver Leth had returned after an absence of five years, and the rumour was that he had news of the Vampaneze Lord! I was in my cell, resting, when word broke. Wasting no time, I pulled on my clothes and hurried to the Hall of Princes at the top of the mountain, to check if the stories were true.

Mika was talking with Paris and Mr Crepsley when I arrived, surrounded by a pack of Generals eager for news. He was clad entirely in black, as was his custom, and his hawk-like eyes seemed darker and grimmer than ever. He raised one gloved hand in salute when he saw me pushing my way forward. I stood to attention and saluted back. "How's the cub Prince?" he asked with a quick, tight grin.

"Not bad," I replied, studying him for signs of injury — many who returned to Vampire Mountain carried the scars of battle. But although Mika looked tired, he hadn't been visibly wounded. "What about the Vampaneze Lord?" I asked directly. "According to the gossip, you know where he is."

Mika grimaced. "If only!" Looking around, he said, "Shall we assemble? I *have* news, but I'd rather announce it to the Hall in general." Everyone present made straight for their seats. Mika settled on his throne and sighed contentedly. "It's good to be back," he said, patting the arms of the hard chair. "Has Seba been taking good care of my coffin?"

"To the vampaneze with your coffin!" a General shouted, momentarily forgetting his place. "What news of the Vampaneze Lord?"

Mika ran a hand through his jet-black hair. "First, let's make it clear — I don't know where he is." A groan spread through the Hall. "But I've had word of him," Mika added, and all ears pricked up at that.

"Before I begin," Mika said, "do you know about the latest vampaneze recruits?" Everybody looked blank. "The vampaneze have been adding to their ranks since the start of the war, blooding more humans than usual, to drive their numbers up."

"This is old news," Paris murmured. "There are far fewer vampaneze than vampires in the world. We expected them to blood recklessly. It is nothing to worry about — we still outnumber them greatly."

"Yes," Mika said. "But now they're also using unblooded humans. They call them 'vampets'. Apparently the Vampaneze

Lord himself came up with the name. Like him, they're learning the rules of vampaneze life and warfare as humans, before being blooded. He plans to build an army of human helpers."

"We can deal with humans," a General snarled, and there were shouts of agreement.

"Normally," Mika agreed. "But we must be wary of these vampets. While they lack the powers of the vampaneze, they're learning to fight like them. Also, since they aren't blooded, they don't have to abide by the more restrictive vampaneze laws. They aren't honour bound to tell the truth, they don't have to follow ancient customs — and they don't have to limit themselves to hand to hand weapons."

Angry mutters swept through the Hall.

"The vampaneze are using *guns*?" Paris asked, shocked. The vampaneze were even stricter than vampires where weapons were involved. We could use boomerangs and spears, but most vampaneze wouldn't touch them.

"The vampets aren't vampaneze," Mika grunted. "There's no reason why a non-blooded vampet shouldn't use a gun. I don't think all their masters approve, but under orders from their Lord, they allow it.

"But the vampets are a problem for another night," Mika continued. "I only mention them now because it's relevant to how I found out about their Lord. A vampaneze would die screaming before betraying his clan, but the vampets aren't so hardened. I captured one a few months ago and squeezed some interesting details out of him.

Foremost of which is — the Vampaneze Lord doesn't have a base. He's travelling the world with a small band of guards, moving among the various fighting units, keeping up morale."

The Generals received the news with great excitement — if the Vampaneze Lord was mobile and lightly protected, he was more vulnerable to attack.

"Did this *vampet* know where the Vampaneze Lord was?" Mr Crepsley asked.

"No," Mika said. "He'd seen him, but that had been more than a year ago. Only those who accompany him know of his travel patterns."

"What else did he tell you?" Paris enquired.

"That their Lord still hasn't been blooded. And that despite his efforts, morale is low. Vampaneze losses are high, and many don't believe they can win the war. There has been talk of a peace treaty — even outright surrender."

Loud cheering broke out. Some Generals were so elated by Mika's words that a group swept forward, picked him up, and carried him from the Hall. They could be heard singing and shouting as they headed for the crates of ale and wine stored below. The other, more sober-headed Generals looked to Paris for guidance.

"Go on," the elderly Prince smiled. "It would be impolite to let Mika and his over-eager companions drink alone."

The remaining Generals applauded the announcement and hurried away, leaving only a few Hall attendants, myself, Mr Crepsley and Paris behind.

"This is foolish," Mr Crepsley grumbled. "If the vampaneze are truly considering surrender, we should push hard after them, not waste time—"

"Larten," Paris interrupted. "Follow the others, find the largest barrel of ale you can, and get good and steaming drunk."

Mr Crepsley stared at the Prince, his mouth wide open. "Paris!" he gasped.

"You have been caged in here too long," Paris said. "Go and unwind, and do not return without a hangover."

"But—" Mr Crepsley began.

"That is an order, Larten," Paris growled.

Mr Crepsley looked as though he'd swallowed a live eel, but he was never one to disobey an order from a superior, so he clicked his heels together, muttered, "Aye, Sire," and stormed off to the store-rooms in a huff.

"I've never seen Mr Crepsley with a hangover," I laughed. "What's he like?"

"Like a … what do the humans say? A gorilla with a sore head?" Paris coughed into a fist — he'd been coughing a lot lately — then smiled. "But it will do him good. Larten takes life too seriously sometimes."

"What about you?" I asked. "Do you want to go?"

Paris pulled a sour face. "A mug of ale would prove the end of me. I shall take advantage of the break by lying in my coffin at the back of the Hall and getting a full day's sleep."

"Are you sure? I can stay if you want."

"No. Go and enjoy yourself. I will be fine."

"OK." I hopped off my throne and made for the door.

"Darren," Paris called me back. "An excessive amount of alcohol is as bad for the young as for the old. If you are wise, you will drink in moderation."

"Remember what you told me about wisdom a few years ago, Paris?" I replied.

"What?"

"You said the only way to get wise was to get experienced." Winking, I rushed out of the Hall and was soon sharing a barrel of ale with a grumpy, orange-haired vampire. Mr Crepsley gradually cheered up as the night progressed, and was singing loudly by the time he reeled back to his coffin late the following morning.

CHAPTER FIVE

I COULDN'T understand why there were two moons in the sky when I awoke, or why they were green. Groaning, I rubbed the back of a hand over my eyes, then looked again. I realized I was lying on the floor, staring up at the green eyes of a chuckling Harkat Mulds. "Have fun last night?" he asked.

"I've been poisoned," I moaned, rolling over on to my stomach, feeling as though I was on the deck of a ship during a fierce storm.

"You won't be wanting boar guts and ... bat broth then?"

"Don't!" I winced, weak at the very thought of food.

"You and the others must have drained ... half the mountain's supply of ale last night," Harkat remarked, helping me to my feet.

"Is there an earthquake?" I asked as he let go of me.

"No," he said, puzzled.

"Then why's the floor shaking?"

He laughed and steered me to my hammock. I'd been sleeping inside the door of our cell. I had vague memories of falling off the hammock every time I tried to get on. "I'll just sit on the floor a while," I said.

"As you wish," Harkat chortled. "Would you like some ale?"

"Go away or I'll hit you," I growled.

"Is ale no longer to your liking?"

"No!"

"That's funny. You were singing about how much you ... loved it earlier. 'Ale, ale, I drink like a whale, I am the ... Prince, the Prince of ale'."

"I could have you tortured," I warned him.

"Never mind," Harkat said. "The whole clan went crazy ... last night. It takes a lot to get a vampire drunk, but ... most managed. I've seen some wandering the tunnels, looking lik—"

"Please," I begged, "don't describe them." Harkat laughed again, pulled me to my feet and led me out of the cell, into the maze of tunnels. "Where are we going?" I asked.

"The Hall of Perta Vin Grahl. I asked Seba about cures ... for hangovers — I had a feeling you'd have one — and he said ... a shower usually did the trick."

"No!" I moaned. "Not the showers! Have mercy!"

Harkat took no notice of my pleas, and soon he was shoving me under the icy cold waters of the internal waterfalls in the Hall of Perta Vin Grahl. I thought my head was going to explode when the water first struck, but after a few minutes the worst of my headache had passed and my stomach had settled. By the time I was towelling myself dry, I felt a hundred times better.

We passed a green-faced Mr Crepsley on our way back to our cell. I bid him a good evening, but he only snarled in reply.

"I'll never understand the appeal of … alcohol," Harkat said as I was dressing.

"Haven't you ever got drunk?" I replied.

"Perhaps in my past life, but not since … becoming a Little Person. I don't have taste buds, and alcohol doesn't … affect me."

"Lucky you," I muttered sourly.

Once I'd dressed, we strolled up to the Hall of Princes to see if Paris needed me, but it was largely deserted and Paris was still in his coffin.

"Let's go on a tour of the tunnels … beneath the Halls," Harkat suggested. We'd done a lot of exploring when we first came to the mountain, but it had been two or three years since we'd last gone off on an adventure.

"Don't you have work to do?" I asked.

"Yes, but…" He frowned. It took a while to get used to Harkat's expressions – it was hard to know whether someone without eyelids and a nose was frowning or grinning – but I'd learnt to read them. "It will hold. I feel strange. I need to be on the move."

"OK," I said. "Let's go walkabout."

We started in the Hall of Corza Jarn, where trainee Generals were taught how to fight. I'd spent many hours here, mastering the use of swords, knives, axes and spears. Most of the weapons were designed for adults, and were too large and cumbersome for me to master, but I'd picked up the basics.

The highest ranking tutor was a blind vampire called Vanez Blane. He'd been my Trials Master during both my Trials of Initiation. He'd lost his left eye in a fight with a lion many decades before, and lost the second six years ago in a fight with the vampaneze.

Vanez was wrestling with three young Generals. Though he was blind, he'd lost none of his sharpness, and the trio ended up flat on their backs in short order at the hands of the ginger-haired games master. "You'll have to learn to do better than that," he told them. Then, with his back to us, he said, "Hello, Darren. Greetings, Harkat Mulds."

"Hi, Vanez," we replied, not surprised that he knew who we were — vampires have very keen senses of smell and hearing.

"I heard you singing last night, Darren," Vanez said, leaving his three students to recover and regroup.

"No!" I gasped, crestfallen. I'd thought Harkat was joking about that.

"Very enlightening," Vanez smiled.

"I didn't!" I groaned. "Tell me I didn't!"

Vanez's smile spread. "I shouldn't worry. Plenty of others made asses of themselves too."

"Ale should be banned," I growled.

"Nothing wrong with ale," Vanez disagreed. "It's the ale-*drinkers* who need to be controlled."

We told Vanez we were going on a tour of the lower tunnels and asked if he'd like to tag along. "Not much point," he said. "I can't see anything. Besides…" Lowering his voice, he told us the three Generals he was training were due to be sent into action soon. "Between ourselves, they're as poor a trio as I've ever passed fit for duty," he sighed. Many vampires were being rushed into the field, to replace casualties in the War of the Scars. It was a contentious point among the clan — it usually took a minimum of twenty years to be declared a General of good standing — but Paris said that desperate times called for desperate measures.

Leaving Vanez, we made for the store-rooms to see Mr Crepsley's old mentor, Seba Nile. At seven hundred, Seba was the second oldest vampire. He dressed in red like Mr Crepsley, and spoke in the same precise way. He was wrinkled and shrunken with age, and limped badly — like Harkat — from a wound to his left leg gained in the same fight that had claimed Vanez's eye.

Seba was delighted to see us. When he heard we were going exploring, he insisted on coming with us. "There is something I wish to show you," he said.

As we left the Halls and entered the vast warren of lower connecting tunnels, I scratched my bald head with my fingernails.

"Ticks?" Seba asked.

"No," I said. "My head's been itching like mad lately. My arms and legs too, and my armpits. I think I have an allergy."

"Allergies are rare among vampires," Seba said. "Let me examine you." Luminous lichen grew along many of the walls and he was able to study me by the light of a thick patch. "Hmmm." He smiled briefly, then released me.

"What is it?" I asked.

"You are coming of age, Master Shan."

"What's that got to do with itching?"

"You will find out," he said mysteriously.

Seba kept stopping at webs to check on spiders. The old quartermaster was uncommonly fond of the eight-legged predators. He didn't keep them as pets, but he spent a lot of time studying their habits and patterns. He was able to communicate with them using his thoughts. Mr Crepsley could too, and so could I.

"Ah!" he said eventually, stopping at a large cobweb. "Here we are." Putting his lips together, he whistled softly, and moments later a big grey spider with curious green spots scuttled down the cobweb and on to Seba's upturned hand.

"Where did that come from?" I asked, stepping forward for a closer look. It was larger than the normal mountain spiders, and different in colour.

"Do you like it?" Seba asked. "I call them Ba'Shan's spiders. I hope you do not object — the name seemed appropriate."

"Ba'Shan's spiders?" I repeated. "Why would—"

I stopped. Fourteen years ago, I'd stolen a poisonous spider from Mr Crepsley — Madam Octa. Eight years later, I'd released her — on Seba's advice — to make a new home with the mountain spiders. Seba said she wouldn't be able to mate with the others. I hadn't seen her since I set her free, and had almost forgotten about her. But now the memory snapped into place, and I knew where this new spider had come from.

"It's one of Madam Octa's, isn't it?" I groaned.

"Yes," Seba said. "She mated with Ba'Halen's spiders. I noticed this new strain three years ago, although it is only this last year that they have multiplied. They are taking over. I think they will become the dominant mountain spider, perhaps within ten or fifteen years."

"Seba!" I snapped. "I only released Madam Octa because you told me she couldn't have offspring. Are they poisonous?"

The quartermaster shrugged. "Yes, but not as deadly as their mother. If four or five attacked together, they could kill, but not one by itself."

"What if they go on a rampage?" I yelled.

"They will not," Seba said stiffly.

"How do you know?"

"I have asked them not to. They are incredibly intelligent, like Madam Octa. They have almost the same mental abilities as rats. I am thinking of training them."

"To do *what*?" I laughed.

"Fight," he said darkly. "Imagine if we could send armies of trained spiders out into the world, with orders to find vampaneze and kill them."

I turned appealingly to Harkat. "Tell him he's crazy. Make him see sense."

Harkat smiled. "It sounds like a good idea … to me," he said.

"Ridiculous!" I snorted. "I'll tell Mika. He hates spiders. He'll send troops down here to stamp them out."

"Please do not," Seba said quietly. "Even if they cannot be trained, I enjoy watching them develop. Please do not rid me of one of my few remaining pleasures."

I sighed and cast my eyes to the ceiling. "OK. I won't tell Mika."

"Nor the others," he pressed. "I would be highly unpopular if word leaked."

"What do you mean?"

Seba cleared his throat guiltily. "The ticks," he muttered. "The new spiders have been feeding on ticks, so they have moved upwards to escape."

"Oh," I said, thinking of all the vampires who'd had to cut their hair and beards and shave under their arms because of the deluge of ticks. I grinned.

"Eventually the spiders will pursue the ticks to the top of the mountain and the epidemic will pass," Seba continued, "but until then I would rather nobody knew what was causing it."

I laughed. "You'd be strung up if this got out!"

"I know," he grimaced.

I promised to keep word of the spiders to myself. Then Seba headed back for the Halls – the short trip had tired him

— and Harkat and me continued down the tunnels. The further we progressed, the quieter Harkat got. He seemed uneasy, but when I asked him what was wrong, he said he didn't know.

Eventually we found a tunnel which led outside. We followed it to where it opened on to the steep mountain face, and sat staring up at the evening sky. It had been months since I'd stuck my head out in the open, and more than two years since I'd slept outdoors. The air tasted fresh and welcome, but strange.

"It's cold," I noted, rubbing my hands up and down my bare arms.

"Is it?" Harkat asked. His dead grey skin only registered extreme degrees of heat or cold.

"It must be late autumn or early winter." It was hard keeping track of the seasons when you lived inside a mountain.

Harkat wasn't listening. He was scanning the forests and valleys below, as if he expected to find someone there.

I walked a short bit down the mountain. Harkat followed, then overtook me and picked up speed. "Careful," I called, but he paid no attention. Soon he was running, and I was left behind, wondering what he was playing at. "Harkat!" I yelled. "You'll trip and crack your skull if you—"

I stopped. He hadn't heard a word. Cursing, I slipped off my shoes, flexed my toes, then started after him. I tried to control my speed, but that wasn't an option on such a steep decline, and soon I was hurtling down the mountain, sending pebbles and dust scattering, yelling at the top of my lungs with excitement and terror.

Somehow we kept on our feet and reached the bottom of the mountain intact. Harkat kept running until he came to a small circle of trees, where he finally stopped and stood as though frozen. I jogged after him and came to a halt. "What … was that … about?" I gasped.

Raising his left hand, Harkat pointed towards the trees.

"What?" I asked, seeing nothing but trunks, branches and leaves.

"He's coming," Harkat hissed.

"Who?"

"The dragon master."

I stared at Harkat oddly. He looked as though he was awake, but perhaps he'd dozed off and was sleepwalking. "I think we should get you back inside," I said, taking his outstretched arm. "We'll find a fire and—"

"Hello, boys!" somebody yelled from within the circle of trees. "Are you the welcoming committee?"

Letting go of Harkat's arm, I stood beside him – now as stiff as he was – and stared again into the cluster of trees. I thought I recognized that voice — though I hoped I was wrong!

Moments later, three figures emerged from the gloom. Two were Little People, who looked almost exactly like Harkat, except they had their hoods up and moved with a stiffness which Harkat had worked out of his system during his years among the vampires. The third was a small, smiling, white-haired man, who struck more fear in me than a band of marauding vampaneze.

Mr Tiny!

After more than six hundred years, Desmond Tiny had returned to Vampire Mountain, and I knew as he strode towards us, beaming like a rat-catcher in league with the Pied Piper of Hamlin, that his reappearance heralded nothing but trouble.

CHAPTER SIX

MR TINY paused briefly when he reached us. The short, plump man was wearing a shabby yellow suit — a thin jacket, no overcoat — with childish-looking green wellington boots and a chunky pair of glasses. The heart-shaped watch he always carried hung by a chain from the front of his jacket. Some said Mr Tiny was an agent of fate — his first name was Desmond, and if you shortened it and put the two names together, you got *Mr Destiny*.

"You've grown, young Shan," he said, running an eye over me. "And you, Harkat..." He smiled at the Little Person, whose green eyes seemed wider and rounder than ever. "*You* have changed beyond recognition. Wearing your hood down, working for vampires — and talking!"

"You knew ... I could talk," Harkat muttered, slipping back into his old broken speech habits. "You always ... knew."

Mr Tiny nodded, then started forward. "Enough of the chit-chat, boys. I have work to do and I must be quick. Time is precious. A volcano's due to erupt on a small tropical island tomorrow. Everybody within a ten-kilometre radius will be roasted alive. I want to be there — it sounds like great fun."

He wasn't joking. That's why everyone feared him — he took pleasure in tragedies which left anyone halfway human shaken to their very core.

We followed Mr Tiny up the mountain, trailed by the two Little People. Harkat looked back often at his 'brothers'. I think he was communicating with them – the Little People can read each other's thoughts – but he said nothing to me about it.

Mr Tiny entered the mountain by a different tunnel to the one we'd used. It was a tunnel I'd never been in, higher, wider and drier than most. There were no twists or side tunnels leading off it. It rose straight and steady up the spine of the mountain. Mr Tiny spotted me staring at the walls of the unfamiliar tunnel. "This is one of my short cuts," he said. "I've short cuts all over the world, in places you wouldn't dream of. Saves time."

As we progressed, we passed groups of very pale-skinned humans in rags, lining the sides of the tunnel, bowing low to Mr Tiny. These were the Guardians of the Blood, people who lived within Vampire Mountain and donated their blood to the vampires. In return, they were allowed to extract a vampire's internal organs and brain when he died — which they ate at special ceremonies!

I felt nervous walking past the ranks of Guardians – I'd never seen so many of them gathered together before – but Mr Tiny only smiled and waved at them, and didn't stop to exchange any words.

Within a quarter of an hour we were at the gate which opened on to the Halls of Vampire Mountain. The guard on duty swung the door wide open when we knocked but stopped when he saw Mr Tiny and half closed it again. "Who are you?" he snapped defensively, hand snaking to the sword on his belt.

"You know who I am, Perlat Cheil," Mr Tiny said, brushing past the startled guard.

"How do you know my–?" Perlat Cheil began, then stopped and gazed after the departing figure. He was trembling and his hand had fallen away from his sword. "Is that who I think it is?" he asked as I passed with Harkat and the Little People.

"Yes," I said simply.

"Charna's guts!" he gasped, and made the death's touch sign by pressing the middle finger of his right hand to his forehead, and the two fingers next to that over his eyelids. It was a sign vampires made when they thought death was close.

Through the tunnels we marched, silencing conversations and causing jaws to drop. Even those who'd never met Mr Tiny recognized him, stopped what they were doing and fell in behind us, following wordlessly, as though trailing a hearse.

There was only one tunnel leading to the Hall of Princes – I'd found another six years ago, but that had since been blocked off – and it was protected by the Mountain's finest guards. They were supposed to stop and search anyone seeking entry to the Hall, but when Mr Tiny approached, they gawped at him, lowered their weapons, then let him – and the rest of the procession – pass unobstructed.

Mr Tiny finally stopped at the doors of the Hall and glanced at the domed building which he'd built six centuries earlier. "It's stood the test of time quite well, hasn't it?" he remarked to no one in particular. Then, laying a hand on the doors, he opened them and entered. Only Princes were supposed to be able to open the doors, but it didn't surprise me that Mr Tiny had the power to control them too.

Mika and Paris were within the Hall, discussing the war with a gaggle of Generals. There were a lot of sore heads and bleary eyes, but everyone snapped to attention when they saw Mr Tiny striding in.

"By the teeth of the gods!" Paris gasped, his face whitening. He cringed as Mr Tiny set foot on the platform of thrones, then drew himself straight and forced a tight smile. "Desmond," he said, "it is good to see you."

"You too, Paris," Mr Tiny responded.

"To what do we owe this unexpected pleasure?" Paris enquired with strained politeness.

"Wait a minute and I'll tell you," Mr Tiny replied, then plopped himself down on a throne – *mine!* – crossed his legs and made himself comfortable. "Get the gang in," he said, crooking a finger at Mika. "I've something to say and it's for everybody's ears."

Within a few minutes, almost every vampire in the mountain had crowded into the Hall of Princes, and stood nervously by the walls – as far away from Mr Tiny as possible – waiting for the mysterious visitor to speak.

Mr Tiny had been checking his nails and rubbing them up and down the front of his jacket. The Little People were standing behind the throne. Harkat stood to their left, looking uncertain. I sensed he didn't know whether to stand with his brothers-of-nature or with his brothers-of-choice — the vampires.

"All present and correct?" Mr Tiny asked. He got to his feet and waddled to the front of the platform. "Then I'll come straight to the point. The Lord of the Vampaneze has been blooded." He paused, anticipating gasps, groans and cries of terror. But we all just stared at him, too shocked to react. "Six hundred years ago," he continued, "I told your forebears that the Vampaneze Lord would lead the vampaneze into a war against you and wipe you out. That was *a* truth — but not *the* truth. The future is both open and closed. There's only one 'will be' but there are often hundreds of 'can be's'. Which means the Vampaneze Lord and his followers *can* be defeated."

Breath caught in every vampire's throat and you could feel hope forming in the air around us, like a cloud.

"The Vampaneze Lord is only a half-vampaneze at the moment," Mr Tiny said. "If you find and kill him before he's fully blooded, victory will be yours."

At that, a huge roar went up, and suddenly vampires were

clapping each other on the back and cheering. A few didn't join in the hooting and hollering. Those with first-hand knowledge of Mr Tiny – myself, Paris, Mr Crepsley – sensed he hadn't finished, and guessed there must be a catch. Mr Tiny wasn't the kind to smile broadly when delivering good news. He only grinned like that when he knew there was going to be suffering and misery.

When the wave of excitement had died down, Mr Tiny raised his right hand. He clutched his heart-shaped watch with his left hand. The watch glowed a dark red colour, and suddenly his right hand glowed as well. All eyes settled on the five crimson fingers and the Hall went eerily quiet.

"When the Vampaneze Lord was discovered seven years ago," Mr Tiny said, his face illuminated by the glow of his fingers, "I studied the strings connecting the present to the future, and saw that there were five chances to avert the course of destiny. One of those has already come and gone."

The red glow faded from his thumb, which he tucked down into his palm. "That chance was Kurda Smahlt," he said. Kurda was the vampire who led the vampaneze against us, in a bid to seize control of the Stone of Blood. "If Kurda had succeeded, most vampires would have been absorbed by the vampaneze and the War of the Scars – as you've termed it – would have been averted.

"But you killed him, destroying what was probably your best hope of survival in the process." He shook his head and tutted. "That was silly."

"Kurda Smahlt was a traitor," Mika growled. "Nothing good comes of treachery. I'd rather die honourably than owe my life to a turncoat."

"More fool you," Mr Tiny chortled, then wiggled his glowing little finger. "This represents your last chance, if all others fail. It will not fall for some time yet – if at all – so we shall ignore it." He tucked the glowing finger down, leaving the three middle fingers standing.

"Which brings us to my reason for coming. If I left you to your own devices, these chances would slip by unnoticed. You'd carry on as you have been, the windows of opportunity would pass, and before you knew it..." He made a soft popping sound.

"Within the next twelve months," he said softly but clearly, "there may be three encounters between certain vampires and the Vampaneze Lord — assuming you heed my advice. Three times he will be at your mercy. If you seize one of these chances and kill him, the war will be yours. If you fail, there'll be one final, all-deciding confrontation, upon which the fate of every living vampire will hang." He paused teasingly. "To be honest, I hope it goes down to the wire — I love big, dramatic conclusions!"

He turned his back on the Hall and one of his Little People handed him a flask, from which he drank deeply. Furious whispers and conversations swept through the assembled vampires while he was drinking, and when he next faced the crowd, Paris Skyle was waiting. "You have been very generous with your information, Desmond," he said. "On behalf of all here, I thank you."

"Don't mention it," Mr Tiny said. His fingers had stopped glowing, he'd let go of his watch, and his hands now rested in his lap.

"Will you extend your generosity and tell us which vampires are destined to encounter the Vampaneze Lord?" Paris asked.

"I will," Mr Tiny said smugly. "But let me make one thing clear — the encounters will only occur if the vampires *choose* to hunt the Lord of the Vampaneze. The three I name don't have to accept the challenge of hunting him down, or take responsibility for the future of the vampire clan. But if they don't, you're doomed, for in these three alone lies the ability to change that which is destined to be."

He slowly looked around the Hall, meeting the eyes of every vampire present, searching for signs of weakness and fear. Not one of us looked away or wilted in the face of such a dire charge. "Very well," he grunted. "One of the hunters is absent, so I'll not name him. If the other two head for the cave of Lady Evanna, they'll probably run into him along the way. If not, his chance to play an active part in the future will pass, and it will boil down to that lone pair."

"And they are...?" Paris asked tensely.

Mr Tiny glanced over at me, and with a horrible sinking feeling in my gut, I guessed what was coming next. "The hunters must be Larten Crepsley and his assistant, Darren Shan," Mr Tiny said simply, and as all eyes in the Hall turned to seek us out, I had the sense of invisible tumblers clicking into place, and knew my years of quiet security inside Vampire Mountain had come to an end.

CHAPTER SEVEN

THE POSSIBILITY of refusing the challenge never entered my thoughts. Six years of living among vampires had filled me with their values and beliefs. Any vampire would lay down his life for the good of the clan. Of course, this wasn't as simple as giving one's life – I had a mission to fulfil, and if I failed, all would suffer – but the principle was the same. I'd been chosen, and a vampire who's been chosen does not say 'no'.

There was a short debate, in which Paris told Mr Crepsley and me that this was not official duty and we didn't have to agree to represent the clan — no shame would befall us if we refused to co-operate with Mr Tiny. At the end of the debate, Mr Crepsley stepped forward, red cloak snapping behind him like wings, and said, "I relish the chance to hunt down the Vampaneze Lord."

I stepped up after him, sorry I wasn't wearing my

impressive blue cloak, and said in what I hoped was a brave tone, "Me too."

"The boy knows how to keep it short," Mr Tiny murmured, winking at Harkat.

"What about the rest of us?" Mika asked. "I've spent five years hunting for that accursed Lord. I wish to accompany them."

"Aye! Me too!" a General in the crowd shouted, and soon everyone was bellowing at Mr Tiny, seeking permission to join us in the hunt.

Mr Tiny shook his head. "Three hunters must seek — no more, no less. Non-vampires may assist them, but if any of their kinsmen tag along, they shall fail."

Angry mutters greeted that statement.

"Why should we believe you?" Mika asked. "Surely ten stand a better chance than three, and twenty more than ten, and thirty—"

Mr Tiny clicked his fingers. There was a sharp, snapping sound and dust fell from overhead. Looking up, I saw long jagged cracks appear in the ceiling of the Hall of Princes. Other vampires saw them too and cried out, alarmed.

"Would you, who has not seen three centuries, dare to tell me, who measures time in continental drifts, about the mechanisms of fate?" Mr Tiny asked menacingly. He clicked his fingers again and the cracks spread. Chunks of the ceiling crumbled inwards. "A thousand vampaneze couldn't chip the walls of this Hall, yet I, by clicking my fingers, can bring it tumbling down." He lifted his fingers to click them again.

"No!" Mika shouted. "I apologize! I didn't mean to offend you!"

Mr Tiny lowered his hand. "Think of this before crossing me again, Mika Ver Leth," he growled, then nodded at the Little People he'd brought with him, who headed for the doors of the Hall. "They'll patch the roof up before we leave," Mr Tiny said. "But next time you anger me, I'll reduce this Hall to rubble, leaving you and your precious Stone of Blood to the whim of the vampaneze."

Blowing dust off his heart-shaped watch, Mr Tiny beamed around the Hall again. "I take it we're decided — three it shall be?"

"Three," Paris agreed.

"Three," Mika muttered bleakly.

"As I said, non-vampires may – indeed, *must* – play a part, but for the next year no vampire should seek out any of the hunters, unless for reasons which have nothing to do with the search for the Vampaneze Lord. Alone they must stand and alone they must succeed or fail."

With that, he brought the meeting to a close. Dismissing Paris and Mika with an arrogant wave of his hand, he beckoned Mr Crepsley and me forward, and grinned at us as he lay back on my throne. He kicked off one of his wellies while he was talking. He wasn't wearing socks, and I was shocked to see he had no toes — his feet were webbed at the ends, with six tiny claws jutting out like a cat's.

"Frightened, Master Shan?" he asked, eyes twinkling mischievously.

"Yes," I said, "but I'm proud to be able to help."

"What if you *aren't* any help?" he jeered. "What if you fail and damn the vampires to extinction?"

I shrugged. "What comes, we take," I said, echoing a saying which was common among the creatures of the night.

Mr Tiny's smile faded. "I preferred you when you were less clever," he grumbled, then looked to Mr Crepsley. "What about you? Scared by the weight of your responsibilities?"

"Yes," Mr Crepsley answered.

"Think you might break beneath it?"

"I might," Mr Crepsley said evenly.

Mr Tiny pulled a face. "You two are no fun. It's impossible to get a rise out of you. Harkat!" he bellowed. Harkat approached automatically. "What do you think of this? Does the fate of the vampires bother you?"

"Yes," Harkat replied. "It does."

"You care for them?" Harkat nodded. "Hmmm." Mr Tiny rubbed his watch, which glowed briefly, then touched the left side of Harkat's head. Harkat gasped and fell to his knees. "You've been having nightmares," Mr Tiny noted, fingers still at Harkat's temple.

"Yes!" Harkat groaned.

"You want them to stop?"

"Yes."

Mr Tiny let go of Harkat, who cried out, then gritted his sharp teeth and stood up straight. Small green tears of pain trickled from the corners of his eyes.

"It's time for you to learn the truth about yourself," Mr Tiny said. "If you come with me, I'll reveal it and the nightmares will stop. If you don't, they'll continue and worsen, and within a year you'll be a screaming wreck."

Harkat trembled at that, but didn't rush to Mr Tiny's side. "If I wait," he said, "will I have ... another chance to learn ... the truth?"

"Yes," Mr Tiny said, "but you'll suffer much in the meantime, and I can't guarantee your safety. If you die before learning who you really are, your soul will be lost forever."

Harkat frowned uncertainly. "I have a feeling," he mumbled. "Something whispers to me— " he touched the left side of his chest "—here. I feel that I should go with Darren ... and Larten."

"If you do, it will improve their chances of defeating the Vampaneze Lord," Mr Tiny said. "Your participation isn't instrumental, but it could be important."

"Harkat," I said softly, "you don't owe us. You've already saved my life twice. Go with Mr Tiny and learn the truth about yourself."

Harkat frowned. "I think that if I ... leave you to learn the truth, the person I was ... won't like what I've done." The Little Person spent a few more difficult seconds brooding about it, then squared up to Mr Tiny. "I'll go with them. Right or wrong, I feel my place is ... with the vampires. All else must wait."

"So be it," Mr Tiny sniffed. "If you survive, our paths will cross again. If not..." His smile was withering.

"What of our search?" Mr Crepsley asked. "You mentioned Lady Evanna. Do we start with her?"

"If you wish," Mr Tiny said. "I can't and won't direct you, but that's where *I* would start. After that, follow your heart. Forget about the quest and go where you feel you belong. Fate will direct you as it pleases."

That was the end of our conversation. Mr Tiny slipped away without a farewell, taking his Little People (they'd completed their repair work while he was talking), no doubt anxious to make that fatal volcano of his the next day.

Vampire Mountain was in uproar that night. Mr Tiny's visit and prophecy were debated and dissected at length. The vampires agreed that Mr Crepsley and me had to leave on our own, to link up with the third hunter – whoever he might be – but were divided as to what the rest of them should do. Some thought that since the clan's future rested with three lone hunters, they should forget the war with the vampaneze, since it no longer seemed to serve any purpose. Most disagreed and said it would be crazy to stop fighting.

Mr Crepsley led Harkat and me from the Hall shortly before dawn, leaving the arguing Princes and Generals behind, saying we needed to get a good day's rest. It was hard to sleep with Mr Tiny's words echoing round my brain, but I managed to squeeze in a few hours.

We woke about three hours before sunset, ate a short meal and packed our meagre belongings (I took a spare set of clothes, some bottles of blood, and my diary). We said private goodbyes to Vanez and Seba — the old quartermaster was especially sad to see us go — then met Paris Skyle at the gate leading out of the Halls. He told us Mika was staying on to assist with the night-to-night running of the war. He looked very poorly as I shook his hand, and I had a feeling that he hadn't many years left — if our search kept us away from Vampire Mountain for a long period, this might be the last time I saw him.

"I'll miss you, Paris," I said, hugging him roughly after we'd shaken hands.

"I will miss you too, young Prince," he said, then squeezed me tight and hissed in my ear: "Find and kill him, Darren. There is a cold chill in my bones, and it is not the chill of old age. Mr Tiny has spoken the truth — if the Vampaneze Lord comes into his full powers, I am sure we all shall perish."

"I'll find him," I vowed, locking gazes with the ancient Prince. "And if the chance falls to me to kill him, my aim will be true."

"Then may the luck of the vampires be with you," he said.

I joined Mr Crepsley and Harkat. We saluted to those who'd gathered to see us off, then faced down the tunnels and set off. We moved quickly and surely, and within two hours had left the mountain and were jogging over open ground, beneath a clear night sky.

Our hunt for the Lord of the Vampaneze had begun!

CHAPTER EIGHT

IT WAS great to be back on the road. We might be walking into the heart of an inferno, and our companions would suffer immeasurably if we failed, but those were worries for the future. In those first few weeks all I could think about was how refreshing it was to stretch my legs and breathe clean air, not caged in with dozens of sweaty, smelly vampires.

I was in high spirits as we cut a path through the mountains by night. Harkat was very quiet and spent a lot of time mulling over what Mr Tiny had said. Mr Crepsley seemed as glum as ever, though I knew that underneath the gloomy façade he was as pleased to be out in the open as I was.

We struck a firm pace and kept to it, covering many kilometres over the course of each night, sleeping deeply by day beneath trees and bushes, or in caves. The cold was fierce when we set off, but as we wound our way down through the mountain range, the biting chill lessened. By the time we reached the lowlands we were as comfortable as a human would have been on a blustery autumn day.

We carried spare bottles of human blood, and fed on wild animals. It had been a long time since I hunted, and I was rusty to begin with, but I soon got back into the swing of it.

"This is the life, isn't it?" I noted one morning as we chewed on the roasted carcass of a deer. We didn't light a fire most days – we ate our meat raw – but it was nice to relax around a mound of blazing logs every once in a while.

"It is," Mr Crepsley agreed.

"I wish we could go on like this forever."

The vampire smiled. "You are not in a hurry to return to Vampire Mountain?"

I pulled a face. "Being a Prince is a great honour, but it's not much fun."

"You have had a rough initiation," he said sympathetically. "Were we not at war, there would have been time for adventure. Most Princes wander the world for decades before settling down to royal duty. Your timing was unfortunate."

"Still, I can't complain," I said cheerfully. "I'm free now."

Harkat stirred up the fire and edged closer towards us. He hadn't said a lot since leaving Vampire Mountain, but now he lowered his mask and spoke. "I loved Vampire Mountain. It felt like home. I never felt so at ease before, even when I ...

was with the Cirque Du Freak. When this is over, if I have ... the choice, I'll return."

"There is vampire blood in you," Mr Crepsley said. He was joking, but Harkat took the statement seriously.

"There might be," he said. "I've often wondered if I was a vampire in ... my previous life. That might explain why I was sent to Vampire Mountain ... and why I fitted in so well. It could also explain the stakes ... in my dreams."

Harkat's dreams often involved stakes. The ground would give way in his nightmares and he'd fall into a pit of stakes, or be chased by shadow men who carried stakes and drove them through his heart.

"Any fresh clues as to who you might have been?" I asked. "Did meeting Mr Tiny jog your memory?"

Harkat shook his chunky, neckless head. "No further insights," he sighed.

"Why did Mr Tiny not tell you the truth about yourself if it was time for you to learn?" Mr Crepsley asked.

"I don't think it's as ... simple as that," Harkat said. "I have to earn the truth. It's part of the ... deal we made."

"Wouldn't it be weird if Harkat *had* been a vampire?" I remarked. "What if he'd been a Prince — would he still be able to open the doors of the Hall of Princes?"

"I don't think I was a Prince," Harkat chuckled, the corners of his wide mouth lifting in a gaping smile.

"Hey," I said, "if *I* can become a Prince, anyone can."

"True," Mr Crepsley muttered, then ducked swiftly as I tossed a leg of deer at him.

Once clear of the mountains, we headed south-east and soon reached the outskirts of civilization. It was strange to see electric lights, cars and planes again. I felt as though I'd been living in the past and had stepped out of a time machine.

"It's so noisy," I commented one night as we passed through a busy town. We'd entered it to draw blood from humans, slicing them in their sleep with our nails, taking a small amount of blood, closing the cuts with Mr Crepsley's healing spit, leaving them oblivious to the fact that they'd been fed upon. "So much music and laughter and shouting." My ears were ringing from the noise.

"Humans always chatter like monkeys," Mr Crepsley said. "It is their way."

I used to object when he said things like that, but not any more. When I became Mr Crepsley's assistant, I'd clung to the hope of returning to my old life. I'd dreamt of regaining my humanity and going home to my family and friends. No longer. My years in Vampire Mountain had rid me of my human desires. I was a creature of the night now — and content to be so.

The itching was getting worse. Before leaving town, I found a pharmacy and bought several anti-itching powders and lotions, which I rubbed into my flesh. The powders and lotions brought no relief. Nothing stopped the itching, and I scratched myself irritably as we journeyed to the cave of Lady Evanna.

Mr Crepsley wouldn't say much about the woman we were

going to meet, where she lived, whether she was a vampire or human, and why we were going to see her.

"You should tell me these things," I grumbled one morning as we made camp. "What if something happens to you? How would Harkat and me find her?"

Mr Crepsley stroked the long scar running down the left side of his face – after all our years together, I still didn't know how he got it – and nodded thoughtfully. "You are right. I will draw a map before nightfall."

"And tell us who she is?"

He hesitated. "That is harder to explain. It might be best coming from her own lips. Evanna tells different people different things. She might not object to you knowing the truth — but then again, she might."

"Is she an inventor?" I pressed. Mr Crepsley owned a collection of pots and pans which folded up into tiny bundles, making them easier to carry. He'd told me that Evanna had made them.

"She sometimes invents," he said. "She is a woman of many talents. Much of her time is spent breeding frogs."

"Excuse me?" I blinked.

"It is her hobby. Some people breed horses, dogs or cats. Evanna breeds frogs."

"How can she breed frogs?" I snorted sceptically.

"You will find out." Then he leant forward and tapped my knee. "Whatever you say, do not call her a witch."

"Why would I call her a witch?" I asked.

"Because she is one — sort of."

"We're going to meet a *witch*?" Harkat snapped worriedly.

"That troubles you?" Mr Crepsley asked.

"Sometimes in my dreams … there's a witch. I've never seen her face — not clearly — and I'm not sure … if she's good or bad. There are times when I run to her for help, and times … when I run away, afraid."

"You haven't mentioned that before," I said.

Harkat's smile was shaky. "With all the dragons, stakes and shadow men … what's one little witch?"

The mention of dragons reminded me of something he'd said when we met Mr Tiny. He'd called him 'the dragon master'. I asked Harkat about this but he couldn't remember saying it. "Although," he mused, "I sometimes see Mr Tiny in my dreams, riding the … backs of dragons. Once he tore the brain out of one and … tossed it at me. I reached to catch it but … woke before I could."

We thought about that image a long time. Vampires place a lot of importance on dreams. Many believe that dreams act as links to the past or future, and that much can be learnt from them. But Harkat's dreams didn't seem to have any bearing on reality, and in the end Mr Crepsley and me dismissed them, rolled over and slept. Harkat didn't — he stayed awake, green eyes glowing faintly, putting off sleep as long as he could, avoiding the dragons, stakes, witches and other perils of his troubled nightmares.

CHAPTER NINE

ONE DUSK I awoke with a feeling of absolute comfort. As I stared up at a red, darkening sky, I tried putting my finger on why I felt so good. Then I realized — the itching had stopped. I lay still a few minutes, afraid it would return if I moved, but when I finally got to my feet, there wasn't the slightest prickling sensation. Grinning, I headed for a small pond we'd camped by, to wet my throat.

I lowered my face into the cool, clear water of the pond and drank deeply. As I was rising, I noticed an unfamiliar face in the reflecting surface of the water — a long-haired, bearded man. It was directly in front of me, which meant he must be standing right behind me — but I hadn't heard anyone approach.

Swivelling swiftly, my hand shot to the sword which I'd brought from Vampire Mountain. I had it halfway out of its scabbard before stopping, confused.

There was no one there.

I looked around for the shabby, bearded man, but he was nowhere to be seen. There were no nearby trees or rocks he could have ducked behind, and not even a vampire could have moved quickly enough to disappear so swiftly.

I turned back towards the pond and looked into the water again. There he was! As clear and hairy as before, scowling up at me.

I gave a yelp and jumped back from the water's edge. Was the bearded man *in* the pond? If so, how was he breathing?

Stepping forward, I locked gazes with the hairy man — he looked like a caveman — for the third time and smiled. He smiled back. "Hello," I said. His lips moved when mine did, but silently. "My name's Darren Shan." Again his lips moved in time with mine. I was getting annoyed — was he mocking me? — when realization struck — it was *me*!

I could see my eyes and the shape of my mouth now that I looked closely, and the small triangular scar just above my right eye, which had become as much a part of me as my nose or ears. It was my face, no doubt about that — but where had all the hair come from?

I felt around my chin and discovered a thick bushy beard. Running my right hand over my head — which should have been smooth — I was stunned to feel long, thick locks of hair. My thumb, which stuck out at an angle, caught in several of the strands, and I winced as I tugged it free, pulling some hair out with it.

What in Khledon Lurt's name had happened to me?

I checked further. Ripping off my T-shirt revealed a chest and stomach covered in hair. Huge balls of hair had also formed under my armpits and over my shoulders. I was hairy all over!

"*Charna's guts!*" I roared, then ran to wake my friends.

Mr Crepsley and Harkat were breaking camp when I rushed up, panting and shouting. The vampire took one look at my hairy figure, whipped out a knife and roared at me to stop. Harkat stepped up beside him, a grim expression on his face. As I halted, gasping for breath, I saw they didn't recognize me. Raising my hands to show they were empty, I croaked, "Don't ... attack! It's ... me!"

Mr Crepsley's eyes widened. "*Darren?*"

"It can't be," Harkat growled. "This is an impostor."

"No!" I moaned. "I woke up, went to the pond to drink, and found ... found..." I shook my hairy arms at them.

Mr Crepsley stepped forward, sheathed his knife, and studied my face incredulously. Then he groaned. "The *purge!*" he muttered.

"The *what?*" I shouted.

"Sit down, Darren," Mr Crepsley said seriously. "We have a lot of talking to do. Harkat — go fill our canteens and fix a new fire."

When Mr Crepsley had gathered his thoughts, he explained to Harkat and me what was happening. "You know that half-vampires become full-vampires when more vampire blood is pumped into them. What we have never discussed —

since I did not anticipate it so soon — is the other way in which one's blood can turn.

"Basically, if one remains a half-vampire for an extremely long period of time — the average is forty years — one's vampire cells eventually attack the human cells and convert them, resulting in full-vampirism. We call this the purge."

"You mean I've become a full-vampire?" I asked quietly, both intrigued and frightened by the notion. Intrigued because it would mean extra strength, the ability to flit and communicate telepathically. Frightened because it would also mean a total retreat from daylight and the world of humanity.

"Not yet," Mr Crepsley said. "The hair is simply the first stage. We shall shave it off presently, and though it will grow back, it will stop after a month or so. You will undergo other changes during that time — you will grow, and experience headaches and sharp bursts of energy — but these too will cease. At the end of the changes, your vampiric blood may have replaced your human blood entirely, but it probably will not, and you will return to normal — for a few months or a couple of years. But sometime within the next few years, your blood *will* turn completely. You have entered the final stages of half-vampirism. There is no turning back."

We spent most of the rest of the night discussing the purge. Mr Crepsley said it was rare for a half-vampire to undergo the purge after less than twenty years, but it was probably linked to when I'd become a Vampire Prince — more vampiric blood had been added to my veins during the ceremony, and that must have speeded up the process.

I recalled Seba studying me in the tunnels of Vampire Mountain, and told Mr Crepsley about it. "He must have known about the purge," I said. "Why didn't he warn me?"

"It was not his place," Mr Crepsley said. "As your mentor, I am responsible for informing you. I am sure he would have told me about it, so that I could have sat down with you and explained it, but there was no time — Mr Tiny arrived and we had to leave the Mountain."

"You said Darren would grow during ... the purge," Harkat said. "How much?"

"There is no telling," Mr Crepsley said. "Potentially, he could mature to adulthood in the space of a few months — but that is unlikely. He shall age a few years, but probably no more."

"You mean I'll finally hit my teens?" I asked.

"I would imagine so."

I thought about that for a while, then grinned. "Cool!"

But the purge was far from cool — it was a curse! Shaving off all the hair was bad enough – Mr Crepsley used a long, sharp blade, which scraped my skin raw – but the changes my body was undergoing were much worse. Bones were lengthening and fusing. My nails and teeth grew – I had to bite my nails and grind my teeth together while I walked at night to keep them in shape – and my feet and hands got longer. Within weeks I was five centimetres taller, aching all over from growth pains.

My senses were in a state of disarray. Slight sounds were magnified — the snapping of a twig was like a house collapsing. The dullest of smells set my nose tingling. My sense of taste deserted me completely. Everything tasted like cardboard. I began to understand what life must be like for Harkat and made a resolution never to tease him about his lack of taste buds again.

Even dim lights were blinding to my ultra-sensitive eye. The moon was like a fierce spotlight in the sky, and if I opened my eyes during the day, I might as well have been sticking two fiery pins into them — the inside of my head would flare with a metallic pain.

"Is this what sunlight is like for full-vampires?" I asked Mr Crepsley one day, as I shivered beneath a thick blanket, eyes shut tight against the painful rays of the sun.

"Yes," he said. "That is why we avoid even short periods of exposure to daylight. The pain of sunburn is not especially great – not for the first ten or fifteen minutes – but the glare of the sun is instantly unbearable."

I suffered with immense headaches during the purge, a result of my out-of-control senses. There were times when I thought my head was going to explode, and I'd weep helplessly from the pain.

Mr Crepsley helped me fight the dizzying effects. He bound light strips of cloth across my eyes – I could still see pretty well – and stuffed balls of grass into my ears and up my nostrils. That was uncomfortable, and I felt ridiculous – Harkat's howls of laughter didn't help – but the headaches lessened.

Another side-effect was a fierce surge of energy. I felt as if I was operating on batteries. I had to run ahead of Mr

Crepsley and Harkat at night, then double back to meet them, just to tire myself out. I exercised like crazy every time we stopped — push-ups, pull-ups, sit-ups — and usually woke long before Mr Crepsley, unable to sleep more than a couple of hours at a time. I climbed trees and cliffs, and swam across rivers and lakes, all in an effort to use up my unnatural store of energy. I'd have wrestled an elephant if I'd found one!

Finally, after six weeks, the turmoil ceased. I stopped growing. I didn't have to shave any more (though the hair on my head remained — I was no longer bald!). I removed the cloth and grass balls, and my taste returned, although patchily to begin with.

I was about seven centimetres taller than I'd been when the purge hit me, and noticeably broader. The skin on my face had hardened, giving me a slightly older appearance — I looked like a fifteen- or sixteen-year-old now.

Most importantly — I was still a half-vampire. The purge hadn't eliminated my human blood cells. The downside of that was I'd have to undergo the discomfort of the purge again in the future. On the plus side I could continue to enjoy sunlight for the time being, before having to abandon it forever in favour of the night.

Although I was keen to become a full-vampire, I'd miss the daytime world. Once my blood turned, there was no going back. I accepted that, but I'd be lying if I said I wasn't nervous. This way, I had months — perhaps a year or two — to prepare myself for the change.

I'd outgrown my clothes and shoes, so I had to stock up at a small human outpost (we were leaving civilization behind again). In an army surplus shop, I chose gear similar to my old stuff, adding a couple of purple shirts to my blue ones, and a dark green pair of trousers. As I was paying for the clothes, a tall, lean man entered. He was wearing a brown shirt, black trousers and a baseball cap. "I need supplies," he grunted at the man serving behind the counter, tossing a list at him.

"You'll need a licence for the guns," the shopkeeper said, running an eye over the scrap of paper.

"I've got one." The man was reaching into a shirt pocket when he caught sight of my hands and stiffened. I was holding my new clothes across my chest, and the scars on my fingertips – where I'd been blooded by Mr Crepsley – were clear.

The man relaxed instantly and turned away — but I was sure he'd recognized the scars and knew what I was. Hurrying from the shop, I found Mr Crepsley and Harkat on the edge of town and told them what had happened.

"Was he nervous?" Mr Crepsley asked. "Did he follow when you left?"

"No. He just went stiff when he saw the marks, then acted as though he hadn't seen them. But he knew what the marks meant — I'm certain of it."

Mr Crepsley rubbed his scar thoughtfully. "Humans who know the truth about vampire marks are uncommon, but some exist. In all probability he is an ordinary person who has simply heard tales of vampires and their fingertips."

"But he *might* be a vampire hunter," I said quietly.

"Vampire hunters are rare — but real." Mr Crepsley thought it over, then decided. "We will proceed as planned, but keep our eyes open, and you or Harkat will remain on watch by day. If an attack comes, we shall be ready." He smiled tightly and touched the handle of his knife. "And waiting!"

CHAPTER TEN

BY DAWN we knew we had a fight on our hands. We were being followed, not just by one person, but three or four. They'd picked up our trail a few kilometres outside the town and had been tracking us ever since. They moved with admirable stealth, and if we hadn't been anticipating trouble, we might not have known anything was amiss. But when a vampire is alert to danger, not even the most fleet-footed human can sneak up on him.

"What's the plan?" Harkat asked as we were making camp in the middle of a small forest, sheltered from the sun beneath the intertwining branches and leaves.

"They will wait for full daylight to attack," Mr Crepsley said, keeping his voice low. "We will act as though all is normal and pretend to sleep. When they come, we deal with them."

"Will you be OK in the sun?" I asked. Though we were

sheltered where we were, a battle might draw us out of the shade.

"The rays will not harm me during the short time it will take to deal with this threat," Mr Crepsley replied. "And I will protect my eyes with cloth, as you did during your purge."

Making beds amid the moss and leaves on the ground, we wrapped ourselves in our cloaks and settled down. "Of course, they might just be curious," Harkat muttered. "They could simply want to see ... what a real-life vampire looks like."

"They move too keenly for that," Mr Crepsley disagreed. "They are here on business."

"I just remembered," I hissed. "The guy in the shop was buying *guns!*"

"Most vampire hunters come properly armed," Mr Crepsley grunted. "Gone are the nights when the fools toted only a hammer and wooden stake."

There was no more talk after that. We lay still, eyes closed (except for Harkat, who covered his lidless eyes with his cloak), breathing evenly, feigning sleep.

Seconds passed slowly, taking an age to become minutes, and an eternity to become hours. It had been six years since my last taste of vicious combat. My limbs felt unnaturally cold, and stiff, icy snakes of fear coiled and uncoiled inside the walls of my stomach. I kept flexing my fingers beneath the folds of my cloak, never far from my sword, ready to draw.

Shortly after midday – when the sun would be most harmful to a vampire – the humans moved in for the kill. There were three of them, spread out in a semicircle. At first I could only hear the rustling of leaves as they approached, and the occasional snap of a twig. But as they closed upon us, I became aware of their heavy breathing, the creak of their tense bones, the pacy, panicked pounding of their hearts.

They came to a standstill ten or twelve metres away, tucked behind trees, preparing themselves to attack. There was a long, nervous pause — then the sound of a gun being slowly cocked.

"Now!" Mr Crepsley roared, springing to his feet, launching himself at the human nearest him.

While Mr Crepsley closed in on his assailant at incredible speed, Harkat and me targeted the others. The one I'd set my sights on cursed loudly, stepped out from behind his tree, brought his rifle up and got a snap shot off. A bullet whizzed past, missing me by several centimetres. Before he could fire again, I was upon him.

I wrenched the rifle from the human's hands and tossed it away. A gun went off behind me, but there was no time to check on my friends. The man in front of me had already drawn a long hunting knife, so I quickly slid my sword out.

The man's eyes widened when he saw the sword – he'd painted the area around his eyes with red circles of what looked like blood – then narrowed. "You're just a kid," he snarled, slashing at me with his knife.

"No," I disagreed, stepping out of range of his knife, jabbing at him with my sword. "I'm much more."

As the human slashed at me again, I brought my sword up and out in a smooth arcing slice, through the flesh, muscles and bones of his right hand, severing three of his fingers, disarming him in an instant.

The human cried out in agony and fell away from me. I took advantage of the moment to see how Mr Crepsley and Harkat were faring. Mr Crepsley had already despatched his human, and was striding towards Harkat, who was wrestling with his opponent. Harkat appeared to have the advantage of his foe, but Mr Crepsley was moving into place to back him up should the battle take a turn for the worse.

Satisfied that all was going in our favour, I switched my attention back to the man on the ground, psyching myself up for the unpleasant task of making an end of him. To my surprise, I found him grinning horribly at me.

"You should have taken my other hand too!" he growled.

My eyes fixed on the man's left hand and my breath caught in my throat — he was clutching a hand grenade close to his chest!

"Don't move!" he shouted as I lurched towards him. He half-pressed down on the detonator with his thumb. "If this goes off, it takes you with me!"

"Easy," I sighed, backing off slightly, gazing fearfully at the primed grenade.

"I'll take it easy in hell," he chuckled sadistically. He'd shaved his head bald and there was a dark 'V' tattooed into either side of his skull, just above his ears. "Now, tell your foul vampire partner and that grey-skinned monster to let my companion go, or I'll—"

There was a sharp whistling sound from the trees to my left. Something struck the grenade and sent it flying from the human's hand. He yelled and grabbed for another grenade (he had a string of them strapped around his chest). There was a second whistling sound and a glinting, multi-pointed object buried itself in the middle of the man's head.

The man slumped backwards with a grunt, shook crazily, then lay still. I stared at him, bewildered, automatically bending closer for a clearer look. The object in his head was a gold throwing star. Neither Mr Crepsley nor Harkat carried such a weapon — so who'd thrown it?

In answer to my unvoiced question, someone jumped from a nearby tree and strode towards me. "Only ever turn your back on a corpse!" the stranger snapped as I whirled towards him. "Didn't Vanez Blane teach you that?"

"I ... forgot," I wheezed, too taken aback to say anything else. The vampire — he had to be one of us — was a burly man of medium height, with reddish skin and dyed green hair, dressed in purple animal hides which had been stitched together crudely. He had huge eyes — almost as large as Harkat's — and a surprisingly small mouth. Unlike Mr Crepsley, his eyes were uncovered, though he was squinting painfully in the sunlight. He wore no shoes and carried no weapons other than dozens of throwing stars strapped to several belts looped around his torso.

"I'll have my shuriken back, thank you," the vampire said to the dead human, prying the throwing star loose, wiping it clean of blood, and reattaching it to one of the belts. He turned the man's head left and right, taking in the shaved skull, tattoos and red circles around the eyes. "A vampet!" he snorted. "I've clashed with them before. Miserable curs." He spat on the dead man, then used his bare foot to roll him over, so he was lying face down.

When the vampire turned to address me, I knew who he was — I'd heard him described many times — and greeted him with the respect he deserved. "Vancha March," I said, bowing my head. "It's an honour to meet you, Sire."

"Likewise," he replied blithely.

Vancha March was the Vampire Prince I'd never met, the wildest and most traditional of all the Princes.

"Vancha!" Mr Crepsley boomed, tearing the cloth away from around his eyes, crossing the space between us and clasping the Prince's shoulders. "What are you doing here, Sire? I thought you were further north."

"I was," Vancha sniffed, freeing his hands and wiping the knuckles of his left hand across his nose, then flicking something green and slimy away. "But there was nothing happening, so I cut south. I'm heading for Lady Evanna's."

"We are too," I said.

"I figured as much. I've been trailing you for the last couple of nights."

"You should have introduced yourself sooner, Sire," Mr Crepsley said.

"This is the first time I've seen the new Prince," Vancha replied. "I wanted to observe him from afar for a while." He studied me sternly. "On the basis of this fight, I have to say I'm not overly impressed!"

"I erred, Sire," I said stiffly. "I was worried about my friends and I made the mistake of pausing when I should have pushed ahead. I accept full responsibility, and I apologize most humbly."

"At least he knows how to make a good apology," Vancha laughed, clapping me on the back.

Vancha March was covered in grime and dirt and smelt like a wolf. It was his standard appearance. Vancha was a true being of the wilds. Even among vampires, he was considered an extremist. He only wore clothes that he'd made himself from wild animal skins, and he never ate cooked meat or drank anything other than fresh water, milk and blood.

As Harkat limped towards us – having finished off his attacker – Vancha sat and crossed his legs. Lifting his left foot, he lowered his head to it and started biting the nails!

"So this is the Little Person who talks," Vancha mumbled, eyeing Harkat over the nail of his left big toe. "Harkat Mulds, isn't it?"

"It is, Sire," Harkat replied, lowering his mask.

"I might as well tell you straight up, Mulds — I don't trust Desmond Tiny or any of his stumpy disciples."

"And I don't trust vampires who … chew their toenails," Harkat threw back at him, then paused and added slyly, "*Sire.*"

Vancha laughed at that and spat out a chunk of nail. "I think we're going to get along fine, Mulds!"

"Hard trek, Sire?" Mr Crepsley asked, sitting down beside the Prince, covering his eyes with cloth again.

"Not bad," Vancha grunted, uncrossing his legs. He then started in on his right toenails. "Yourselves?"

"The travelling has been good."

"Any news from Vampire Mountain?" Vancha asked.

"Lots," Mr Crepsley said.

"Save it for tonight." Vancha let go of his foot and lay back. He took off his purple cloak and draped it over himself. "Wake me when it's dusk," he yawned, rolled over, fell straight asleep and started to snore.

I stared, goggle-eyed, at the sleeping Prince, then at the nails he'd chewed off and spat out, then at his ragged clothes and dirty green hair, then at Harkat and Mr Crepsley. "*He's* a Vampire Prince?" I whispered.

"He is," Mr Crepsley smiled.

"But he looks like…" Harkat muttered uncertainly. "He acts like…"

"Do not be fooled by appearances," Mr Crepsley said. "Vancha chooses to live roughly, but he is the finest of vampires."

"If you say so," I responded dubiously, and spent most of the day lying on my back, staring up at the cloudy sky, kept awake by the loud snoring of Vancha March.

CHAPTER ELEVEN

WE LEFT the vampets lying where we'd killed them (Vancha said they weren't worthy of burial) and set off at dusk. As we marched, Mr Crepsley told the Prince of Mr Tiny's visit to Vampire Mountain, and what he'd predicted. Vancha said little while Mr Crepsley was talking, and brooded upon his words in silence for a long time after he finished.

"I don't think it takes a genius to surmise that I'm the third hunter," he said in the end.

"I would be most surprised if you were not," Mr Crepsley agreed.

Vancha had been picking between his teeth with the tip of a sharp twig. Now he tossed it aside and spat into the dust of the trail. Vancha was a master spitter — his spit was thick, globular and green, and he could hit an ant at twenty paces. "I don't trust that evil meddler, Tiny," he snapped. "I've run into him a couple of times, and I've made a habit of doing the opposite of anything he says."

Mr Crepsley nodded. "Generally speaking, I would agree with you. But these are dangerous times, Sire, and–"

"Larten!" the Prince interrupted. "It's 'Vancha', 'March' or 'Hey, ugly!' while we're on the trail. I won't have you kowtowing to me."

"Very well–" Mr Crepsley grinned "–*ugly*." He grew serious again. "These are dangerous times, Vancha. The future of our race is at stake. Dare we ignore Mr Tiny's prophecy? If there is hope, we must seize it."

Vancha let out a long, unhappy sigh. "For hundreds of years, Tiny's let us think we were doomed to lose the war when the Vampaneze Lord arose. Why does he tell us now, after all this time, that it *isn't* cut and dried, but we can *only* prevent it if we follow his instructions?" The Prince scratched the back of his neck and spat into the bush to our left. "It sounds like a load of guano to me!"

"Maybe Evanna can shed light on the subject," Mr Crepsley said. "She shares some of Mr Tiny's powers and can sense the paths of the future. She might be able to confirm or dismiss his predictions."

"If so, I'll believe her," Vancha said. "Evanna guards her tongue closely, but when she speaks, she speaks the truth. If she says our destiny lies on the road, I'll gladly pitch in with you. If not…" He shrugged and let the matter rest.

Vancha March was *weird* — and that was putting it mildly! I'd never met anyone like him. He had a code all of his own.

As I already knew, he wouldn't eat cooked meat or drink anything but fresh water, milk and blood, and he made his clothes from the hides of animals he hunted. But I learnt much more about him during the six nights it took us to reach Lady Evanna's.

He followed the old ways of the vampires. Long ago, vampires believed that we were descended from wolves. If we lived good lives and stayed true to our beliefs, we'd become wolves again when we died and roam the wilds of Paradise as spirit creatures of the eternal night. To that end, they lived more like wolves than humans, avoiding civilization except when they had to drink blood, making their own clothes, following the laws of the wild.

Vancha wouldn't sleep in a coffin — he said they were too comfortable! He thought a vampire should sleep on open ground, covering himself with no more than his cloak. He respected vampires who used coffins but had a very low opinion of those who slept in beds. I didn't dare tell him about my preference for hammocks!

He had a great interest in dreams, and often ate wild mushrooms which led to vibrant dreams and visions. He believed the future was mapped out in our dreams, and if we learnt to decipher them, we could control our destinies. He was fascinated by Harkat's nightmares and spent many long hours discussing them with the Little Person.

The only weapons he used were his shurikens (the throwing stars), which he carved himself from various metals and stones. He thought hand to hand combat should be exactly that — fought with one's hands. He'd no time for swords, spears or axes and refused to touch them.

"But how can you fight someone who has a sword?" I asked one evening as we were getting ready to break camp. "Do you run?"

"I run from nothing!" he replied sharply. "Here — let me show you." Rubbing his hands together, he stood opposite me and told me to draw my sword. When I hesitated, he slapped my left shoulder and jeered. "Afraid?"

"Of course not," I snapped. "I just don't want to hurt you."

He laughed out loud. "There's not much fear of that, is there, Larten?"

"I would not be so sure," Mr Crepsley demurred. "Darren is only a half-vampire but he is sharp. He could test you, Vancha."

"Good," the Prince said. "I relish worthy opponents."

I looked pleadingly at Mr Crepsley. "I don't want to draw on an unarmed man."

"*Unarmed?*" Vancha shouted. "I have *two* arms!" He waved them at me.

"Go ahead," Mr Crepsley said. "Vancha knows what he is doing."

Pulling out my sword, I faced Vancha and made a half-hearted lunge. He didn't move. Simply watched as I pulled the tip of my sword up short.

"Pathetic," he sniffed.

"This is stupid," I told him. "I'm not–"

Before I could say anything else, he darted forward, seized me by the throat and made a small, painful cut across my neck with his nails.

"Ow!" I yelled, stumbling away from him.

"Next time I'll cut your nose off," he said pleasantly.

"No you won't!" I growled and swung at him with my sword, properly this time.

Vancha ducked clear of the arc of the blade. "Good," he grinned. "That's more like it."

He circled me, eyes on mine, fingers flexing slowly. I kept the tip of my sword low, until he came to a halt, then moved towards him and jabbed. I expected him to shift aside, but instead he brought the palm of his right hand up and swiped the blade away, as he would a flat stick. As I struggled to bring it back around, he stepped in, caught hold of my hand above the wrist, gave a sharp twist which caused me to release the sword — and I was weaponless.

"See?" he smiled, stepping back and raising his hands to show the fight was at an end. "If this was for real, your ass would be grass." Vancha had a foul mouth — that was one of his tamest insults!

"Big deal," I sulked, rubbing my sore wrist. "You beat a half-vampire. You couldn't win against a full-vampire or a vampaneze."

"I can and have," he insisted. "Weapons are tools of fear, used by those who are afraid. One who learns to fight with his hands always has the advantage over those who rely on swords and knives. Know why?"

"Why?"

"Because *they* expect to win," he beamed. "Weapons are false — they're not of nature — and inspire false confidence. When I fight, I expect to die. Even now, when I sparred with you, I anticipated death and resigned myself to it. Death is the worst this world can throw at you, Darren — if you accept it, it has no power over you."

Picking up my sword, he handed it to me and watched to see what I'd do. I had the feeling he wanted me to cast it aside — and I was tempted to, to earn his respect. But I'd have felt naked without it, so I slid it back into its sheath and glanced down at the ground, slightly ashamed.

Vancha clasped the back of my neck and squeezed amiably. "Don't let it bother you," he said. "You're young. You have loads of time to learn." His eyes creased as he thought about Mr Tiny and the Lord of the Vampaneze, and he added gloomily, "I hope."

I asked Vancha to teach me how to fight bare-handed. I'd studied unarmed combat in Vampire Mountain, but that had been against opponents who were also unarmed. Apart from a few lessons regarding what to do if I lost my weapon during battle, I'd never been taught how to take on a fully armed foe using only my hands. Vancha said it would take years to master, and I could expect lots of nicks and bruises while learning. I waved away such concerns — I loved the thought of being able to best an armed vampaneze with my bare hands.

Training couldn't start on the trail, but Vancha talked me through a few basic blocking tactics when we rested by day, and promised to give me a real work out when we got to Evanna's.

The Prince would tell me no more about the witch than Mr Crepsley had, though he did say she was both the fairest and least attractive of women — which made no sense at all!

I thought Vancha would be strongly anti-vampaneze — the vampires who despised vampaneze the most were normally those steeped in the old ways — but to my surprise he had nothing against them. "Vampaneze are noble and true," he said a couple of nights before we reached Evanna's. "I don't agree with their feeding habits — there's no need to kill when we drink — but otherwise I admire them."

"Vancha nominated Kurda Smahlt to become a Prince," Mr Crepsley remarked.

"I admired Kurda," Vancha said. "He was known for his brains, but he also had guts. He was a remarkable vampire."

"Don't you..." I coughed and trailed off into silence.

"Say what's on your mind," Vancha told me.

"Don't you feel bad for nominating him, after what he did, leading the vampaneze against us?"

"No," Vancha said bluntly. "I don't approve of his actions, and if I'd been at Council, I wouldn't have spoken up on his behalf. But he was following his heart. He acted for the good of the clan. Misguided as he was, I don't think Kurda was a real traitor. He acted poorly, but his motives were pure."

"I agree," Harkat said, joining the conversation. "I think Kurda's been poorly treated. It was right that he was killed when he … was captured, but it's wrong to say he was a villain, and not mention his name … in the Hall of Princes."

I didn't respond to that. I'd liked Kurda immensely, and knew he'd done his best to spare the vampires the wrath of the Vampaneze Lord. But he'd killed one of my other friends – Gavner Purl – and brought about the death of more, including Arra Sails, a female vampire who'd once been Mr Crepsley's mate.

I learnt the identity of Vancha's *real* enemy the day before we came to the end of the first leg of our journey. I'd been sleeping, but my face was itchy – an after-effect of the purge – and I awoke before midday. I sat up, scratching under my chin, and spotted Vancha at the edge of camp, his clothes tossed aside – except for a strip of bear hide tied around his waist – rubbing spit into his skin.

"Vancha?" I asked quietly. "What are you doing?"

"I'm going walking," he said, and continued rubbing spit into the flesh of his shoulders and arms.

I stared up at the sky. It was a bright day and hardly any clouds were around to block out the sun. "Vancha, it's *daytime*," I said.

"Really?" he replied sarcastically. "I'd never have guessed."

"Vampires burn in sunlight," I said, wondering if he'd bumped his head and forgotten what he was.

"Not immediately," he said, then looked at me sharply. "Have you ever wondered *why* vampires burn in the sun?"

"Well, no, not exactly…"

"There's no logical reason," Vancha said. "According to the stories humans tell, it's because we're evil, and evil beings can't face the sun. But that's nonsense — we're not evil, and even if we were, we should still be able to move about during the day.

"Look at wolves," he continued. "We're supposed to be descended from them, but they can endure the sunlight. Even true nocturnal creatures like bats and owls can survive by day. Sunlight might confuse them, but it doesn't kill them. *So why does it kill vampires?*"

I shook my head uncertainly. "I don't know. Why?"

Vancha barked a laugh. "Damned if I know! Nobody does. Some claim we were cursed by a witch or sorcerer, but I doubt that — the world's full of servants of the dark arts, but none with the power to make such a lethal curse. My hunch is Desmond Tiny."

"What's Mr Tiny got to do with it?" I asked.

"According to ancient legends – forgotten by most – Tiny created the first vampires. They say he experimented on wolves and mixed their blood with that of humans, resulting in…" He tapped his chest.

"That's ridiculous," I snorted.

"Perhaps. But if those legends are true, our sun-related weakness is also Tiny's work. They say he was afraid we'd grow too powerful and take over the world, so he tainted our blood and made us slaves of the night." He stopped rubbing spit in and gazed upwards, eyes scrunched up against the disorientating rays of sunlight. "Nothing's as awful as slavery," he said quietly. "If the stories are true, and we're night slaves because of Tiny's meddling, there's only one way to win back our freedom — *fight*! We have to take on the enemy, look it full in the face and spit in its eye."

"You mean fight Mr Tiny?"

"Not directly. He's too slippery a customer to pin down."

"Then who?"

"We have to fight his manservant," he said. When I looked blank, he elaborated: "The sun."

"The *sun*?" I laughed, then stopped when I saw he was serious. "How can you fight the sun?"

"Simple," Vancha said. "You face it, take its blows, and keep coming back for more. For years I've been subjecting myself to the rays of the sun. Every few weeks I walk about for an hour by day, letting the sun burn me, toughening my skin and eyes to it, testing it, seeing how long I can survive."

"You're crazy!" I chortled. "Do you really think you can get the better of the sun?"

"I don't see why not," he said. "A foe's a foe. If it can be engaged, it can be defeated."

"Have you made any progress?" I asked.

"Not really," he sighed. "It's much the same as when I began. The light half-blinds me — it takes almost a full day for my vision to return to normal and the headaches to fade. The rays cause a reddening within ten or fifteen minutes, and it gets painful soon after. I've managed to endure it for close to eighty minutes a couple of times, but I'm badly burnt by the end, and it takes five or six nights of total rest to recover."

"When did this war of yours begin?"

"Let's see," he mused. "I was about two hundred when I started—" Most vampires weren't sure of their exact age; when you lived as long as they did, birthdays ceased to mean very much "—and I'm more than three hundred now, so I guess it's been the best part of a century."

"A hundred years!" I gasped. "Have you ever heard the phrase, 'banging your head against a brick wall'?"

"Of course," he smirked, "but you forget, Darren — vampires can break walls with their heads!"

With that, he winked and walked off into the sunlight, whistling loudly, to engage in his crazy battle with a huge ball of burning gas hanging millions and millions of kilometres away in the sky.

CHAPTER TWELVE

A FULL moon was shining when we arrived at Lady Evanna's. Even so, I'd have missed the clearing if Mr Crepsley hadn't nudged me and said, "We are here." I later learnt that Evanna had cast a masking spell over the place, so unless you knew where to look, your eyes would skim over her home and not register it.

I stared straight ahead, but for a few seconds could see nothing but trees. Then the power of the spell faded, the imaginary trees 'vanished' and I found myself gazing down upon a crystal-clear pond, glowing a faint white colour from the light of the moon. There was a hill on the opposite side of the pond, and I could see the dark, arched entrance of a huge cave in it.

As we strolled down the gentle slope to the pond, the night air filled with the sound of croaking. I stopped, alarmed, but Vancha smiled and said, "Frogs. They're alerting Evanna. They'll stop once she tells them it's safe."

Moments later the frog chorus ceased and we walked in silence again. We skirted the edge of the pond, Mr Crepsley and Vancha warning Harkat and me not to step on any frogs, thousands of which were at rest by or in the cool water.

"The frogs are creepy," Harkat whispered. "I feel like they're ... watching us."

"They are," Vancha said. "They guard the pond and cave, protecting Evanna from intruders."

"What could a bunch of frogs do against intruders?" I laughed.

Vancha stooped and grabbed a frog. Holding it up to the moonlight, he gently squeezed its sides. Its mouth opened and a long tongue darted out. Vancha caught the tongue with the index finger and thumb of his right hand, careful not to touch the edges. "See the tiny sacs along the sides?" he asked.

"Those yellow-red bulges?" I said. "What about them?"

"Filled with poison. If this frog wrapped its tongue around your arm or the calf of your leg, the sacs would pop and the poison would seep in through your flesh." He shook his head grimly. "Death in thirty seconds."

Vancha laid the frog down on the damp grass and let go of its tongue. It hopped away about its business. Harkat and me walked with extreme care after that!

When we reached the mouth of the cave, we stopped. Mr Crepsley and Vancha sat down and laid aside their packs. Vancha took out a bone he'd been chewing on for the last couple of nights and got to work on it, pausing only to spit at the occasional frog which wandered too close to us.

"Aren't we going in?" I asked.

"Not without being invited," Mr Crepsley replied. "Evanna does not take kindly to intruders."

"Isn't there a bell we can ring?"

"Evanna has no need of bells," he said. "She knows we are here and will come to greet us in her own time."

"Evanna's not a lady to be rushed," Vancha agreed. "A friend of mine thought he'd enter the cave on the quiet once, to surprise her." He munched cheerfully on his bone. "She gave him huge warts all over. He looked like ... like..." Vancha frowned. "It's hard to say, because I've never seen anything quite like it — and I've seen most everything in my time!"

"Should we be here if she's that dangerous?" I asked worriedly.

"Evanna will not harm us," Mr Crepsley assured me. "She has a quick temper, and it's best not to rile her, but she would never kill one with vampire blood, unless provoked."

"Just make sure you don't call her a witch," Vancha warned, for what must have been the hundredth time.

Half an hour after we'd settled by the cave, dozens of frogs — larger than those surrounding the pond — came hopping out. They formed a circle around us and sat, blinking slowly, hemming us in. I started to get to my feet, but Mr Crepsley told me to stay seated. Moments later, a woman emerged from the cave. She was the ugliest, most unkempt woman I'd ever seen. She was short — barely taller than the squat Harkat Mulds — with long, dark, untidy hair.

She had rippling muscles and thick, strong legs. Her ears were sharply pointed, her nose was tiny — it looked like there were just two holes above her upper lip — and her eyes were narrow. When she got closer, I saw that one eye was brown and the other green. What was even stranger was that the colours switched — one minute her left eye would be brown, the next her right.

She was extraordinarily hairy. Her arms and legs were covered with black hair; her eyebrows were two large caterpillars; bushy hair grew out of her ears and nostrils; she had a fairly full beard, and her moustache would have put Otto von Bismarck to shame.

Her fingers were surprisingly stubby. As a witch, I'd expected her to have bony claws, though I guess that's an image I got from books and comics I read when I was a child. Her nails were cut short, except for on the two little fingers, where they grew long and sharp.

She didn't wear traditional clothes, or animal hides like Vancha. Instead she dressed in *ropes*. Long, thickly woven, yellow ropes, wrapped around her chest and lower body, leaving her arms, legs and stomach free.

I'd have found it hard to imagine a more fearsome, off-putting woman, and my insides gurgled uneasily as she shuffled towards us.

"Vampires!" she snorted, stepping through the ranks of frogs, which parted as she advanced. "Always ugly bloody vampires! Why don't handsome humans ever come a-calling?"

"They're probably afraid you'd eat them," Vancha laughed in reply, then stood and hugged her. She hugged back, hard, and lifted the Vampire Prince off his feet.

"My little Vancha," she cooed, as though cuddling a baby. "You've put on some weight, Sire."

"And you're uglier than ever, Lady," he grunted, gasping for breath.

"You're only saying that to please me," she giggled, then dropped him and turned to Mr Crepsley. "Larten," she nodded politely.

"Evanna," he replied, standing and bowing. Then, without warning, he kicked out at her. But, swift as he was, the witch was swifter. She grabbed his leg and twisted. He rolled over and collapsed flat on the ground. Before he could react, Evanna jumped on his back, grabbed his chin and pulled his head up sharply.

"Surrender?" she yelled.

"Yes!" he wheezed, face reddening — not with shame, but pain.

"Wise boy," she laughed, and kissed his forehead quickly.

Then she stood and studied Harkat and me, running a curious green eye over Harkat and a brown one over me.

"Lady Evanna," I said as warmly as I could, trying not to let my teeth chatter.

"It is good to meet you, Darren Shan," she replied. "You are welcome."

"Lady," Harkat said, bowing politely. He wasn't as nervous as me.

"Hello, Harkat," she said, returning Harkat's bow. "You are also welcome — as you were before."

"*Before?*" he echoed.

"This is not your first visit," she said. "You have changed in many ways, within and without, but I recognize you. I'm gifted that way. Appearances don't deceive me for long."

"You mean … you know who I was … before I became a Little Person?" Harkat asked, astonished. When Evanna nodded, he leant forward eagerly. "Who was I?"

The witch shook her head. "Can't say. That's for you to find out."

Harkat wanted to push the matter, but before he could, she fixed her gaze on me and stepped forward to cup my chin between several cold, rough fingers. "So this is the boy Prince," she murmured, turning my head left, then right. "I thought you would be younger."

"He was struck by the purge as we travelled here," Mr Crepsley informed her.

"That explains it." She hadn't let go of my face and still her eyes scanned me, as though probing for weakness.

"So," I said, feeling as though I should speak, saying the first thing that popped into my head, "you're a witch, are you?"

Mr Crepsley and Vancha groaned.

Evanna's nostrils flared and her head shot forward so our faces were millimetres apart. "*What* did you call me?" she hissed.

"Um. Nothing. Sorry. I didn't mean it. I–"

"You two are to blame!" she roared, spinning away from me to face a wincing Mr Crepsley and Vancha March. "You told him I was a witch!"

"No, Evanna," Vancha said quickly.

"We told him *not* to call you that," Mr Crepsley assured her.

"I should gut the pair of you," Evanna growled, cocking the little finger of her right hand at them. "I would, too, if Darren wasn't here — but I'd hate to make a bad first impression." Glowering hotly, she relaxed her little finger. Mr Crepsley and Vancha relaxed too. I could barely believe it. I'd seen Mr Crepsley face fully armed vampaneze without flinching, and was sure Vancha was every bit as composed in the face of great danger. Yet here they stood, trembling before a short, ugly woman with nothing more threatening than a couple of long fingernails!

I started to laugh at the vampires, but then Evanna whirled around and the laughter died on my lips. Her face had changed and she now looked more like an animal than a human, with a huge mouth and long fangs. I took a frightened step back. "Mind the frogs!" Harkat shouted, grabbing my arm to stop me stepping on one of the poisonous guards.

I glanced down to make sure I hadn't trodden on any frogs. When I looked up again, Evanna's face was back to normal. She was smiling. "Appearances, Darren," she said. "Never let them fool you." The air around her shimmered. When it cleared, she was tall, lithe and beautiful, with golden hair and a flowing white gown. My jaw dropped and I stared at her rudely, astonished by how pretty she was.

She clicked her fingers and was her original self again. "I'm a sorceress," she said. "A wyrd sister. An enchantress. A priestess of the arcane. I am not–" she added, shooting a piercing look at Mr Crepsley and Vancha, "–a *witch*. I'm a creature of many magical talents. These allow me to take any shape I choose — at least in the minds of those who see me."

"Then why..." I started to say, before remembering my manners.

"...do I choose this ugly form?" she finished for me. Blushing, I nodded. "I feel comfortable this way. Beauty means nothing to me. Looks are the least important thing in my world. This is the shape I assumed when I first took human form, so it is the shape I return to most often."

"I prefer you when you're beautiful," Vancha muttered, then coughed gruffly when he realized he'd spoken aloud.

"Be careful, Vancha," Evanna chuckled, "or I'll take my hand to you as I did to Larten all those years ago." She cocked an eyebrow at me. "Did he ever tell you how he got that scar?"

I looked at the long scar running down the left side of Mr Crepsley's face, and shook my head. The vampire was blushing a deep crimson colour. "Please, Lady," he pleaded. "Do not speak of it. I was young and foolish."

"You most certainly were," Evanna agreed, and nudged me wickedly in the ribs. "I was wearing one of my beautiful faces. Larten got tipsy on wine and tried to kiss me. I gave him a little scratch to teach him some manners."

I was stunned. I'd always thought he picked up the scar fighting vampaneze or some fierce animal of the wilds!

"You are cruel, Evanna," Mr Crepsley moped, stroking his scar miserably.

Vancha was laughing so hard that snot was streaming from his nose. "Larten!" he howled. "Wait till I tell the others! I always wondered why you were so coy about that scar. Normally vampires boast about their wounds, but you—"

"Shut up!" Mr Crepsley snapped with uncharacteristic bluntness.

"I could have healed it," Evanna said. "If it had been stitched immediately, it wouldn't be half as noticeable as it is. But he took off like a kicked dog and didn't return for thirty years."

"I did not feel wanted," Mr Crepsley said softly.

"Poor Larten," she smirked. "You thought you were a real ladies' man when you were a young vampire, but..." She pulled a face and cursed. "I knew I'd forgotten something. I meant to have them set up when you arrived, but I got distracted." Muttering to herself, she turned to the frogs and made low, croaking noises.

"What's she doing?" I asked Vancha.

"Talking to the frogs," he said. He was still grinning about Mr Crepsley's scar.

Harkat gasped and dropped to his knees. "Darren!" he called, pointing to a frog. Crouching beside him, I saw that on the back of the frog was an eerily accurate image of Paris Skyle, done in dark green and black.

"Weird," I said, and gently touched the image, ready to whip my hand back if the frog opened its mouth. I frowned and traced the lines more firmly. "Hey," I said, "this isn't paint. I think it's a birthmark"

"It can't be," Harkat said. "No birthmark could look that … much like a person, especially not one we– Hey! There's another!"

I turned and looked where he was pointing. "That's not Paris," I said.

"No," Harkat agreed, "but it's a face. And there's a third." He pointed to a different frog.

"And a fourth," I noted, standing and gazing around.

"They *must* be painted on," Harkat said.

"They're not," Vancha said. Bending, he picked up a frog and held it out for us to examine. This close to it, aided by the strong light of the moon, we could see that the marks were actually underneath the frog's uppermost layer of skin.

"I told you Evanna bred frogs," Mr Crepsley reminded us. He took the frog from Vancha and traced the shape of the face, which was burly and bearded. "It is a mix of nature and magic. She finds frogs with strong natural markings, magically enhances them, and breeds them, producing faces. She is the only one in the world who can do it."

"Here we are," Evanna said, pushing Vancha and me aside, leading nine frogs over to Mr Crepsley. "I feel guilty for lumbering you with that scar, Larten. I shouldn't have cut so deeply."

"It is forgotten, Lady," he smiled gently. "The scar is part of me now. I am proud of it–" he glared at Vancha "–even if others can only mock."

"Still," she said, "it irks me. I've presented you with gifts over the years – such as the collapsible pots and pans – but they haven't satisfied me."

"There is no need–" Mr Crepsley began.

"Shut up and let me finish!" she growled. "I think at last I have a gift which will restore amends. It's not something you can take, just a little … token."

Mr Crepsley looked down at the frogs. "I hope you do not mean to give the frogs to me."

"Not exactly." She croaked an order to the frogs and they rearranged themselves. "I know Arra Sails was killed in the fighting with the vampaneze six years ago," she said. Mr Crepsley's face dropped at the mention of Arra's name. He'd been very close to her and had taken her death hard.

"She died valiantly," he said.

"I don't suppose you kept anything of hers, did you?"

"Such as?"

"A lock of hair, a knife which was dear to her, a scrap of her clothes?"

"Vampires do not indulge in such foolishness," he said gruffly.

"They should," Evanna sighed. The frogs stopped moving, she looked down at them, nodded and stepped aside.

"What are—" Mr Crepsley began, then fell silent as his eyes took in the frogs and the huge face spread across their backs.

It was the face of Arra Sails, a section on each frog's back. The face was perfect in every detail and boasted more colour than the faces on the other frogs — Evanna had worked in yellows, blues and reds, bringing life to its eyes, cheeks, lips and hair. Vampires can't be photographed — their atoms bounce around in a bizarre way, impossible to capture on film — but this was as close to a photo of Arra Sails as was imaginable.

Mr Crepsley hadn't moved. His mouth was a tight line across the lower half of his face, but his eyes were filled with warmth, sadness and ... love.

"Thank you, Evanna," he whispered.

"No need," she smiled softly, then looked around at the rest of us. "I think we should leave him alone a while. Come into the cave."

Wordlessly we followed her in. Even the normally raucous Vancha March was quiet, pausing only to clasp Mr Crepsley's left shoulder and squeeze comfortingly. The frogs hopped along after us, except the nine with Arra's features plastered across their backs. They stayed, held their shape and kept Mr Crepsley company as he gazed sorrowfully at the face of his one-time mate and dwelt at length upon the painful past.

CHAPTER THIRTEEN

EVANNA HAD prepared a feast for us, but it was all vegetables and fruit — she was a vegetarian and wouldn't allow anyone to eat meat in her cave. Vancha teased her about it — "Still on the cow-food, Lady?" — but ate his share along with Harkat and me, though he only chose food which hadn't been cooked.

"How can you eat that?" I asked, revolted, as he tucked into a raw turnip.

"All in the conditioning," he winked, biting deeply into it. "Yum — a worm!"

Mr Crepsley joined us as we were finishing. He was in a sombre mood for the rest of the night, saying little, staring off into space.

The cave was far more luxurious than the caverns of Vampire Mountain. Evanna had made a real home of it, with soft feather beds, wonderful paintings on the walls and huge candle-lit lamps which cast a rosy glow over everything. There were couches to lie on, fans to cool us, exotic fruit and wine. After so many years of rough living, it seemed like a palace.

As we relaxed and digested the meal, Vancha cleared his throat and broached our reason for being here. "Evanna, we've come to discuss—"

She silenced him with a quick wave of a hand. "We'll have none of that tonight," she insisted. "Official business can wait until tomorrow. This is a time for friendship and rest."

"Very well, Lady. This is your domain and I bow to your wishes." Lying back, Vancha burped loudly, then looked for somewhere to spit. Evanna tossed a small silver pot at him. "Ah!" he beamed. "A spittoon." He leant over and spat forcefully into it. There was a slight 'ping' and Vancha grunted happily.

"I was cleaning up for days the last time he visited," Evanna remarked to Harkat and me. "Pools of spit everywhere. Hopefully the spittoon will keep him in order. Now if only there was something for him to flick his nose-pickings into..."

"Are you complaining about me?" Vancha asked.

"Of course not, Sire," she replied sarcastically. "What woman could object to a man invading her home and covering the floor with mucus?"

"I don't think of you as a woman, Evanna," he laughed.

"Oh?" There was ice in her tone. "What *do* you think of me as?"

"A witch," he said innocently, then leapt from the couch and raced out of the cave before she cast a spell on him.

Later, when Evanna had regained her sense of humour, Vancha snuck back in to his couch, fluffed up a cushion, stretched out and chewed at a wart on his left palm.

"I thought you only slept on the floor," I remarked.

"Ordinarily," he agreed, "but it'd be impolite to refuse another's hospitality, especially when your host is the Lady of the Wilds."

I sat up curiously. "Why do you call her a Lady? Is she a princess?"

Vancha's laughter echoed through the cave. "Do you hear that, Lady? The boy thinks you're a princess!"

"What's so strange about that?" she asked, stroking her moustache. "Don't all princesses look like this?"

"Beneath Paradise, perhaps," Vancha chuckled. Vampires believe that the souls of good vampires go beyond the stars to Paradise when they die. There isn't such a thing as hell in vampire mythology – most believe the souls of bad vampires stay trapped on Earth – but occasionally one would refer to a 'beneath Paradise'.

"No," Vancha said seriously. "Evanna's far more important and regal than any mere princess."

"Why, Vancha," she cooed, "that was almost flattering."

"I can flatter when I want," he said, then broke wind loudly. "And flutter too!"

"Disgusting," Evanna sneered, but she had a hard time hiding a smile.

"Darren was asking about you on the way here," Vancha said to Evanna. "We told him nothing of your past. Would you care to fill him in?"

Evanna shook her head. "You tell it, Vancha. I'm not in the mood for story-telling. But keep it short," she added, as he opened his mouth to begin.

"I will," he promised.

"And don't be rude."

"Lady Evanna!" he gasped. "Am I ever?" Grinning, he ran a hand through his green hair, thought a while, then began in a soft voice which I hadn't heard him use before. "Heed, children," he said, then cocked an eyebrow and said in his own voice, "That's the way to begin a story. Humans start with 'Once upon a time', but what do humans know about—"

"Vancha," Evanna interrupted. "I said keep it short."

Vancha grimaced, then started over, again in his soft voice. "Heed, children — we creatures of the night were not made to beget heirs. Our women can't give birth and our men can't sire children. This is the way it's been since the first vampire walked by the light of the moon, and the way we thought it would always be.

"But seventeen hundred years ago, there lived a vampire by the name of Corza Jarn. He was ordinary in all respects, making his way in the world, until he fell in love and mated with a vampiress called Sarfa Grall. They were happy, hunting and fighting side by side, and when the first term of their mating agreement elapsed, they agreed to mate again."

That's how vampire 'marriages' work. Vampires don't agree to stay with one another for life, only for ten, fifteen or twenty years. Once that time is up, they can agree to another decade or two together, or go their separate ways.

"Midway through their second term," Vancha continued, "Corza grew restless. He wished to have a baby with Sarfa and raise a child of his own. He refused to accept their natural limitations and went looking for the cure to vampire sterility. For decades he searched in vain, the loyal Sarfa by his side. A hundred years came and went. Two hundred. Sarfa died during the quest but this didn't put Corza off — if anything, it made him search even harder for a solution. Finally, fourteen hundred years ago, his search led him to that meddler with the watch — Desmond Tiny.

"Now," Vancha said gruffly, "it's not known exactly how much power Mr Tiny wields over vampires. Some say he created us, others that he once was one of us, others still that he's simply an interested observer. Corza Jarn knew no more about Tiny's true self than the rest, but he believed the magician could help, and followed him around the world, begging him to put an end to the barren curse of the vampire clan.

"For two centuries Mr Tiny laughed at Corza Jarn and waved his pleas away. He told the vampire — now old and feeble, close to death — to stop worrying. He said children weren't meant for vampires. Corza wouldn't accept this. He pestered Tiny and begged him to give the vampires hope. He offered his soul in exchange for a solution, but Mr Tiny sneered and said if he wanted Corza's soul, he would simply take it."

"I haven't heard that part of the story before," Evanna cut in.

Vancha shrugged. "Legends are flexible. I think it's good to remind people of Tiny's cruel nature, so I do, every chance I get.

"Eventually," he returned to the story, "for reasons of his own, Tiny relented. He said he'd create a woman capable of bearing a vampire's child, but added a catch — the woman and her children would either make the clan more powerful than ever ... or destroy us completely!

"Corza was troubled by Tiny's words, but he'd sought too long and hard to be dissuaded by the threat. He agreed to Tiny's terms, and let him take some of his blood. Tiny mixed Corza's blood with that of a pregnant wolf and worked strange charms on her. The wolf gave birth to four cubs. Two were stillborn and normal in shape, but the others were alive — and human in appearance! One was a boy, the other a *girl*."

Vancha paused and looked at Evanna. Harkat and me looked too, our eyes wide. The witch grimaced, then stood and took a bow. "Yes," she said, "*I* was that hairy little she-cub."

"The children grew quickly," Vancha went on. "Within a year they were adults and left their mother and Corza, to seek out their destiny in the wilds. The boy went first, without saying anything, and nobody knows what became of him.

"Before the girl left, she gave Corza a message to take to the clan. He was to tell them what had happened, and say that she took her duties very seriously. He was also to tell them that she was not ready for motherhood, and that no vampire should seek her out as a mate. She said there was much she had to consider, and it would be centuries – perhaps longer – before she made her choice.

"That was the last any vampire saw of her for four hundred years."

He stopped, looked thoughtful for a moment, then picked up a banana and began to eat it, skin and all. "The end," he mumbled.

"The *end*?" I shouted. "It can't end there! What happened next? What did she do for those four centuries? Did she choose a mate when she came back?"

"She chose no mate," Vancha said. "Still hasn't. As for what she got up to…" He smiled. "Maybe you should ask her yourselves."

Harkat and me turned to Evanna. "*Well?*" we asked together.

Evanna pursed her lips. "I chose a name," she said.

I laughed. "You can't have spent four hundred years picking a name!"

"That wasn't all I got up to," she agreed, "but I devoted much of that time to the choice. Names are vital to beings of destiny. I have a role to play in the future, not just of the vampire clan, but of every creature in the world. The name I chose would have a bearing on that role. I settled in the end for Evanna." She paused. "I *think* it was a good choice."

Rising, Evanna croaked something at her frogs, who set off for the mouth of the cave. "I must go," she said. "We have spoken enough of the past. I will be absent most of the day. When I return, we shall discuss your quest and the part I am to take in it." She departed after the frogs, and moments later had disappeared into the ripening rays of the dawn.

Harkat and me stared after her. Then Harkat asked Vancha if the legend he'd told was true. "As true as any legend can be," Vancha replied cheerfully.

"What does that mean?" Harkat asked.

"Legends change in the telling," Vancha said. "Seventeen hundred years is a long time, even by vampire standards. Did Corza Jarn really drag around the world after Desmond Tiny? Did that agent of chaos agree to help? Could Evanna and the boy have been born of a she-wolf?" He scratched an armpit, sniffed his fingers and sighed. "Only three people in the world know the truth — Desmond Tiny, the boy – if he still lives – and Lady Evanna."

"Have you ever asked Evanna if it's true?" Harkat enquired.

Vancha shook his head. "I've always preferred a stirring good legend to boring old facts." With that, the Prince rolled over and dropped off to sleep, leaving Harkat and me to discuss the story quietly and wonder.

CHAPTER FOURTEEN

I AROSE with Vancha a couple of hours after midday and commenced my training in the shade near the cave entrance. Harkat watched us with interest, as did Mr Crepsley when he woke early that afternoon. Vancha started me off with a stick, saying it would be months before he tried me with real weapons. I spent the afternoon watching him flick and stab the stick at me. I didn't have to do anything else, just observe the movements of the stick and learn to identify and anticipate the various ways an attacker had of using it.

We practised until Evanna returned, half an hour shy of sunset. She said nothing of where she'd been or what she'd been up to, and nobody enquired.

"Having fun?" she asked, entering the cave with her entourage of frogs.

"Heaps," Vancha replied, throwing the stick away. "The boy wants to learn to fight with his hands."

"Are swords too heavy for him?"

Vancha pulled a face. "Very funny."

Evanna's laughter brightened the cave. "I'm sorry. But fighting with hands – or swords – seems so childish. People should battle with their brains."

I frowned. "How?"

Evanna glanced at me, and all of a sudden the strength went from my legs and I fell to the floor. "What's happening?" I squealed, flopping about like a dying fish. "What's wrong with me?"

"Nothing," Evanna said, and to my relief my legs returned to normal. "*That's* how you fight with your brain," she said as I gathered myself together. "Every part of the body connects to the brain. Nothing functions without it. Attack with your brain, and victory is all but assured."

"Could I learn to do that?" I asked eagerly.

"Yes," Evanna said. "But it would take a few hundred years and you would have to leave the vampires and become my assistant." She smiled. "What do you think, Darren? Would it be worth it?"

"I'm not sure," I muttered. I liked the idea of learning magic, but living with Evanna wasn't appealing — with her quick temper, I doubted she'd make an understanding or forgiving teacher!

"Let me know if you change your mind," she said. "It's been a long time since I had an assistant, and none ever completed their studies — they all ran off after a few years, though I can't imagine why." Evanna brushed past us into the cave. Moments later she called us, and when we entered, we found another feast waiting.

"Did you use magic to get it ready so quickly?" I asked, sitting down to eat.

"No," she replied. "I simply moved a little faster than normal. I can work at quite a speed when I wish."

We ate a big dinner, then sat around a fire and discussed Mr Tiny's visit to Vampire Mountain. Evanna seemed to know about it already, but let us tell the story and said nothing until we had finished. "The three hunters," she mused once we'd brought her up to date. "I have been waiting for you for many centuries."

"You have?" Mr Crepsley asked, startled.

"I lack Desmond's clear insight into the future," she said, "but I see some of what is to come — or what *might* come. I knew three hunters would emerge to face the Vampaneze Lord, but I didn't know who they'd be."

"Do you know if we'll be successful?" Vancha asked, observing her keenly.

"I doubt if even Desmond knows that," she said. "Two strong futures lie ahead, each as possible as the other. It's rare for fate to boil down to two such evenly matched eventualities. Normally the paths of the future are many. When two exist like this, chance decides which the world will take."

"What about the Lord of the Vampaneze?" Mr Crepsley asked. "Have you any idea where he is?"

"Yes." Evanna smiled.

Mr Crepsley's breath caught in his throat.

"But you won't tell us, will you?" Vancha snorted in disgust.

"No," she said, her smile spreading. Her teeth were long, jagged and yellow like a wolf's.

"Will you tell us how we are to find him?" Mr Crepsley asked. "And when?"

"I cannot," Evanna said. "If I told, I would change the course of the future, and that's not allowed. You must search for him yourselves. I will accompany you on the next leg of your journey, but I cannot—"

"You're coming with us?" Vancha exploded in astonishment.

"Yes. But only as a travelling companion. I'll play no part in the quest to find the Vampaneze Lord."

Vancha and Mr Crepsley exchanged uneasy looks.

"You have never travelled with vampires before, Lady," Mr Crepsley said.

Evanna laughed. "I know how important I am to your people, and for that reason I've avoided too much contact with the children of the night — I tire of vampires pleading with me to mate with them and have their babies."

"Then why come with us now?" Vancha asked bluntly.

"There's someone I wish to meet," she answered. "I could seek him alone, but I prefer not to. My reasons will become clear in time."

"Witches are so bloody secretive," Vancha grumbled, but Evanna didn't rise to the bait.

"If you prefer to travel without me, you may," she said. "I will not impose my presence upon you."

"We would be honoured to have you as an escort, Lady Evanna," Mr Crepsley assured her. "And please do not take offence if we appear suspicious or unwelcoming — these are troublesome, confusing times, and we bark where sometimes we should whisper."

"Well put, Larten," she smiled. "If that's settled, I'll pack my things and we'll take to the road."

"So soon?" Mr Crepsley blinked.

"Now is as good a time as ever."

"I hope the frogs aren't coming," Vancha huffed.

"I wasn't going to bring them," Evanna said, "but now that you mention it…" She laughed at his expression. "Don't worry — my frogs will stay and keep things tidy for when I return." She started to leave, paused, turned slowly and squatted. "One more thing," she said, and by her serious expression we knew something bad was coming. "Desmond should have told you this, but he obviously chose not to — playing mind games, no doubt."

"What is it, Lady?" Vancha asked when she paused.

"It concerns the hunt for the Vampaneze Lord. I don't know whether you'll succeed or fail, but I have seen into the future of each possible outcome and gleaned some facts of what lies in store.

"I will not speak of the future where you succeed — it is not for me to comment on that — but if you fail…" Again she stalled. Reaching out, she took both of Vancha's hands in her left — it seemed to have grown incredibly large — and Mr Crepsley's in her right. While she held hands with them, she locked gazes with me, and spoke. "I tell you this because I think you should know. I don't say it to frighten you, but to prepare you, should matters come to the worst.

"Four times your paths are fated to cross with that of the Vampaneze Lord. If they do cross, on each occasion you will have it within your power to make an end of him. If you fail, the vampaneze are destined to win the War of the Scars. This you already know.

"But what Desmond didn't tell you is — by the end of the hunt, if you have faced the Vampaneze Lord four times and failed to kill him, only one of you will be alive to witness the fall of the vampire clan." Lowering her gaze and removing her hands from Mr Crepsley's and Vancha's, she said in something less than a whisper, "The other two will be *dead.*"

CHAPTER FIFTEEN

WE SOLEMNLY filed out of Evanna's cave and circled the pond, each of us brooding about the witch's prophecy. We'd known from the start that this would be a peril-filled quest, with death never far from our heels. But it's one thing to anticipate your possible end, quite another to be told it's a certainty if you fail.

We followed no particular direction that first night, only walked aimlessly through the darkness, saying nothing, barely taking note of our surroundings. Harkat hadn't been included in Evanna's prophecy – he wasn't one of the hunters – but was as disturbed as the rest of us.

Towards dawn, as we were making camp, Vancha suddenly burst out laughing. "Look at us!" he hooted, as we stared at him uncertainly. "We've been moping all night like four sad souls at a funeral. What idiots we've been!"

"You think it amusing to have a death sentence imposed on us, Sire?" Mr Crepsley asked archly.

"Charna's guts!" Vancha cursed. "The sentence has been there since the start — all that's changed is that we know about it!"

"A little knowledge is a ... dangerous thing," Harkat muttered.

"That's a human way of thinking," Vancha chided him. "I'd rather know what lies ahead, good or bad. Evanna has done us a favour by telling us."

"How do you figure that?" I asked.

"She confirmed that we'll have four chances to kill the Vampaneze Lord. Think about it — four times his life will be ours to take. Four times we'll face him and do battle. He might get the better of us once. Perhaps twice. But do you really think he'll evade us four times in a row?"

"He will not be alone," Mr Crepsley said. "He travels with guards, and all vampaneze in the area will rush to his aid."

"What makes you think that?" Vancha challenged him.

"He is their Lord. They will sacrifice their lives to protect him."

"Will our fellow vampires back us up if *we* run into trouble?" Vancha responded.

"No, but that is because..." Mr Crepsley stopped.

"...Mr Tiny's told them not to," Vancha grinned. "And if he's picked just three vampires to go head to head with the Vampaneze Lord, maybe–"

"–he has only picked three vampaneze to help their Lord!" Mr Crepsley finished, excited.

"Right," Vancha beamed. "So the odds against us besting him are, in my view, better than even. Do you agree?" All three of us nodded thoughtfully. "Now," he continued, "let's say we make a pig's ear of it. We face him four times, we blow it, and our chance to defeat him passes. What happens then?"

"He leads the vampaneze into war against the vampires and wins," I said.

"Exactly." Vancha's smile faded. "By the way, I don't believe that. I don't care how powerful their Lord is, or what Des Tiny says — in a war with the vampaneze, I'm certain we'll win. But if we don't, I'd rather die beforehand, fighting for our future, than be there to watch the walls of our world come crashing down."

"Brave words," I grunted sourly.

"The truth," Vancha insisted. "Would you prefer to die at the hands of the Vampaneze Lord, when hope is still on our side, or survive and bear witness to the downfall of the clan?" I didn't reply, so Vancha went on. "If the predictions are true, and we fail, I don't want to be around for the end. It would be a terrible tragedy, and would madden anyone who saw it.

"Believe me," Vancha said, "the two who die in that eventuality will be fortunate. We shouldn't worry about dying — it's *living* we have to fear if we fail!"

I didn't get much sleep that day, thinking about what Vancha had said. I doubt if any of us slept much, except Evanna, who snored even louder than the Prince.

Vancha was right. If we failed, the one who survived would have the worst time of all. He'd have to watch the vampires perish, and bear the burden of blame. If we were to fail, death along the way was the best any of us could hope for.

Our spirits had lifted when we rose that evening. We were no longer afraid of what lay ahead, and instead of talking negatively, we discussed our route. "Mr Tiny said to follow our hearts," Mr Crepsley reminded us. "He said fate would lead us if we placed ourselves in its hands."

"You don't think we should try tracking down the Vampaneze Lord?" Vancha asked.

"Our people have spent six years seeking him, without success," Mr Crepsley said. "Of course we must keep our eyes peeled, but otherwise I believe we should go about our business as if he did not exist."

"I don't like it," Vancha grumbled. "Fate's a cruel mistress. What if destiny doesn't lead us to him? Do you want to report back in a year and say, 'Sorry, we didn't run into the blighter, bad luck, what?'"

"Mr Tiny said to follow our hearts," Mr Crepsley repeated stubbornly.

Vancha threw his hands into the air. "OK — we'll do it your way. But you two will have to pick the course — as many women have attested, I'm a boundless cad who doesn't have a heart."

Mr Crepsley smiled thinly. "Darren? Where do you want to go?"

I started to say I didn't care, then stopped as an image flashed through my thoughts — a picture of a snake-boy sticking an extra long tongue up his nose. "I'd like to see how Evra's doing," I said.

Mr Crepsley nodded approvingly. "Good. Just last night I was wondering what my old friend Hibernius Tall was up to. Harkat?"

"Sounds good to me," Harkat agreed.

"So be it." Facing Vancha, Mr Crepsley said in as imperious a tone as he could muster, "Sire, we head for the Cirque Du Freak."

And so our direction was decided and the dice of destiny were cast.

CHAPTER SIXTEEN

MR CREPSLEY was able to tap into Mr Tall's thoughts and pinpoint the position of the Cirque Du Freak. The travelling circus was relatively near, and it would take us only three weeks to link up with it if we forced the pace.

After a week, we hit civilization again. As we passed a small town one night, I asked Mr Crepsley why we didn't hop on a bus or train, which would get us to the Cirque Du Freak much quicker. "Vancha does not approve of human modes of transport," he said. "He has never been in a car or on a train."

"*Never?*" I asked the barefooted Prince.

"I wouldn't even spit on a car," he said. "Awful things. The shape, the noise, the smell." He shivered.

"What about planes?"

"If the gods of the vampires meant for us to fly," he said, "they'd have given us wings."

"What about you, Evanna?" Harkat asked. "Have you ever flown?"

"Only on a broomstick," she said. I didn't know if she was joking or not.

"And you, Larten?" Harkat asked.

"Once, long ago, when the Wright brothers were just getting going." He paused. "It crashed. Luckily, it had not been flying very high, so I was not seriously injured. But these new contraptions, which soar above the clouds … I think not."

"Afraid?" I smirked.

"Once bitten, twice shy," he replied.

We were a strange group, no doubt about it. We had almost nothing in common with humans. They were creatures of the technological age, but we belonged to the past — vampires knew nothing of computers, satellite dishes, microwave ovens, or any other modern conveniences; we travelled by foot most of the time, had simple tastes and pleasures, and hunted as animals. Where humans sent aeroplanes to wage their wars and fought by pressing buttons, we battled with swords and our hands. Vampires and humans might share the same planet, but we lived in different worlds.

I awoke one afternoon to the sound of Harkat's moans. He was having another nightmare and was tossing feverishly about on the grassy bank where he'd fallen asleep. I leant over to wake him. "Hold," Evanna said. The witch was in the lower branches of a tree, observing Harkat with unseemly interest. A squirrel was exploring her head of long hair, and another was chewing on the ropes she used as clothes.

"He's having a nightmare," I said.

"He has them often?"

"Almost every time he sleeps. I'm supposed to wake him if I hear him having one." I bent to shake him awake.

"Hold," Evanna said again, jumping down. She shuffled over and touched the three middle fingers of her right hand to Harkat's forehead. She closed her eyes and crouched there a minute, then opened them and let go. "Dragons," she said. "Bad dreams. His time of insight is upon him. Did Desmond say nothing about revealing who Harkat was in his previous life?"

"Yes, but Harkat chose to come with us, to search for the Vampaneze Lord."

"Noble but foolish," she mused.

"If you told him who he was, would that ease his nightmares?"

"No. He must learn the truth himself. I'd make things worse if I meddled. But there is a way to temporarily ease his pain."

"How?" I asked.

"One who speaks the language of the dragons could help."

"Where will we find someone like that?" I snorted, then paused. "Can you...?" I left the question hanging.

"Not I," she said. "I can talk to many animals, but not dragons. Only those who have bonded with the flying reptiles can speak their language." She stood. "*You* could help."

"Me?" I frowned. "I haven't bonded with a dragon. I've never even seen one. I thought they were imaginary."

"In this time and place, they are," Evanna agreed. "But there are other times and places, and bonds can be formed unknown."

That didn't make sense, but if I could somehow help Harkat, I would. "Tell me what I have to do," I said.

Evanna smiled approvingly, then told me to lay my hands on Harkat's head and close my eyes. "Focus," she said. "We need to find an image for you to fix upon. How about the Stone of Blood? Can you picture it, red and throbbing, the blood of the vampires flowing through its mysterious veins?"

"Yes," I said, bringing the stone effortlessly to mind.

"Keep thinking of it. In a few minutes you'll experience unpleasant sensations, and maybe catch glimpses of Harkat's nightmares. Ignore them and stay focused on the Stone. I will do the rest."

I did as she said. At first it was easy, but then I began to feel strange. The air around me seemed to get hotter and it became harder to breathe. I heard the beating of immense wings, then caught a glimpse of something dropping from a blood-red sky. I cringed, almost let go of Harkat, but remembered Evanna's advice and forced myself to focus on the image of the Stone of Blood.

I sensed something huge land behind me, and felt hot eyes boring into my back, but I didn't turn or shrink away. I reminded myself that this was a dream, an illusion, and thought about the Stone.

Harkat appeared before me in the vision, stretched upon a bed of stakes, which impaled him all over. He was alive but in incredible pain. He couldn't see me — the tips of two stakes poked out of the sockets where his eyes should have been.

"His pain is nothing to what *you* will feel," someone said, and looking up I saw a figure of shadows, elusive and dark, hovering close by.

"Who are you?" I gasped, momentarily forgetting about the Stone.

"I am the Lord of the Crimson Night," he replied mockingly.

"The Lord of the Vampaneze?" I asked.

"Of them and all others," the shadow man jeered. "I have been waiting for you, Prince of the Damned. Now I have you — and I won't let go!" The shadow man darted forward, his fingers ten long claws of dark menace. Red eyes glowed in the black pit that was his face. For a terrifying moment I thought he was going to grab and devour me. Then a tiny voice — Evanna's — whispered, "It's just a dream. He can't hurt you, not yet, not if you focus on the Stone."

Shutting my eyes within the dream, I ignored the charge of the shadow man and concentrated on the pulsing Stone of Blood. There was a hissing scream and I felt as though a wave of frothing madness had broken over me. Then the nightmare faded and I was back in the real world.

"You can open your eyes now," Evanna said. My eyes snapped open. I let go of Harkat and wiped my hands over my face, reacting as though I'd been touched by something dirty. "You did well," Evanna congratulated me.

"That ... *thing*," I gasped. "What was it?"

"The Lord of Destruction," she said. "The Master of Shadows. The would-be ruler of the eternal night."

"He was so powerful, so evil."

She nodded. "He will be."

"*Will be?*" I echoed.

"What you saw was a shade of the future. The Lord of the Shadows has not yet come into his own, but he will, eventually. This cannot be avoided, and you should not worry about it. All that matters for the time being is that your friend will sleep untroubled now."

I glanced down at Harkat, who was resting peacefully. "He's OK?"

"He will be, for a time," Evanna said. "The nightmares will return, and when they do he'll have to face his past and learn who he was, or succumb to madness. But for now he can sleep soundly, unafraid."

She headed back to her tree.

"Evanna," I stopped her with a soft call. "This Lord of the Shadows... There was something familiar about him. I couldn't make out his face, but I felt I knew him."

"So you should," she whispered in reply. She hesitated, pondering how much to tell me. "What I say now is between you and me," she warned. "It must go no further. You can tell no one, not even Larten or Vancha."

"I won't," I promised.

Keeping her back to me, she said, "The future is dark, Darren. There are two paths, and both are winding and troubled, paved with the souls of the dead. In one of the possible futures, the Vampaneze Lord has become the Master of Shadows and ruler of the dark. In the other..."

She paused, and her head tilted backwards, as though she was staring up at the sky for an answer. "In the other, the Lord of the Shadows is *you.*"

And she departed, leaving me confused and shaken, dearly wishing that Harkat's moans hadn't woken me up.

A couple of nights later, we hooked up with the Cirque Du Freak.

Mr Tall and his band of magical performers were playing outside a small village, in an abandoned church. The show was drawing to a close when we arrived, so we slipped inside and watched the finale from the back. Sive and Seersa – the twisting twins – were onstage, twirling around each other and performing incredible acrobatic stunts. Mr Tall came on after them, dressed in a dark suit, with his customary red hat and gloves, and said the show was over. People began to leave, many muttering about the weak finish, when two snakes slid down from the rafters, sending waves of fear rippling through the crowd.

I grinned when I saw the snakes. This was how most of the shows drew to a close. People were tricked into thinking the show was over, then the snakes appeared and gave the crowd one last scare. Before the serpents could do any damage, Evra Von – their master – would step in and calm them down.

Sure enough, as the snakes were about to slither on to the floor, Evra stepped forward. But he wasn't alone — there was a small child with him, who went to one of the snakes and controlled it as Evra controlled the other. The kid was a new addition. I assumed Mr Tall had picked him up on his travels.

After Evra and the boy had wrapped the snakes around themselves, Mr Tall came on again and said the show was over for real. We kept to the shadows while the crowd streamed past, chattering with excitement. Then, as Evra and the child unwound and brushed themselves down, I moved. "Evra Von!" I roared.

Evra whirled around, startled. "Who's there?" I didn't answer, but walked forward briskly. His eyes widened with astonished delight. *"Darren!"* he yelled, and threw his arms around me. I hugged him tightly, ignoring the feel of his slippery scales, delighted to see him after so many years. "Where have you been?" he cried when we let go of one another. There were tears of happiness in his eyes — mine were wet too.

"Vampire Mountain," I said lightly. "How about you?"

"All over the world." He studied me curiously. "You've grown."

"Only recently. And not as much as you." Evra was a man now. He was only a few years older than me, and we'd looked much the same age when I first joined the Cirque Du Freak, but now he could have passed for my father.

"Good evening, Evra Von," Mr Crepsley said, stepping forward to shake hands.

"Larten," Evra nodded. "It's been a long time. I'm glad to see you."

Mr Crepsley stood to one side and introduced our companions. "I would like you to meet Vancha March, Lady Evanna, and Harkat Mulds, whom I believe you already know."

"Hello," Vancha grunted.

"Greetings," Evanna smiled.

"Hi, Evra," Harkat said.

Evra blinked. "It spoke!" he gasped.

"Harkat speaks a lot these nights," I grinned.

"It has a name?"

"It has," Harkat said. "And 'it' would like very much … to be called 'he'."

Evra didn't know what to say. When I'd lived with him, we'd spent a lot of our time gathering food for the Little People, and never once had one of them said a word. We thought they couldn't speak. Now here I was with a Little Person – the limping one, whom we'd nicknamed Lefty – acting as if his being able to talk was no big deal.

"Welcome back to the Cirque Du Freak, Darren," somebody said, and looking up I found myself face to belly button with Mr Tall. I'd forgotten how quickly and silently the owner of the Cirque could move.

"Mr Tall," I replied, nodding politely (he didn't like to shake hands).

He greeted the others by name, including Harkat. When Harkat returned the greeting, Mr Tall didn't look in the least surprised. "Would you care to eat?" he asked us.

"That would be delightful," Evanna answered. "And I would have a word or two with you afterwards, Hibernius. There are things we must discuss."

"Yes," he agreed without batting an eyelid. "There are."

As we filed out of the church, I fell in step with Evra to discuss old times. He was carrying his snake over his shoulders. The boy who'd performed with Evra caught up with us as we exited, dragging the other snake behind him like a toy. "Darren," Evra said, "I'd like you to meet Shancus."

"Hello, Shancus," I said, shaking the boy's hand.

"'Lo," he replied. He had the same yellow, green hair, narrow eyes, and multicoloured scales as Evra. "Are you the Darren Shan I was named after?" he asked.

I glanced sideways at Evra. "Am I?"

"Yes," he laughed. "Shancus was my first-born. I thought it would be—"

"*First-born?*" I interrupted. "He's *yours?* You're his *father?*"

"I certainly hope so," Evra grinned.

"But he's so big! So old!"

Shancus preened proudly at the remark.

"He'll be five soon," Evra said. "He's large for his age. I started him out in the act a couple of months ago. He's a natural."

This was bizarre! Of course, Evra was old enough to be married with kids, and there was no reason for me to be surprised by the news — but it seemed like only a few months since we'd been hanging out together as teenagers, wondering what life would be like when we grew up.

"You've got other children?" I asked.

"A couple," he said. "Urcha — three — and Lilia, who'll be two next month."

"Are they all snake-children?"

"Urcha isn't. He's upset — he wants scales too — but we try to make him feel as loved and extraordinary as the others."

"'*We*' being...?"

"Me and Merla. You don't know her. She joined the show shortly after you left — ours was a whirlwind romance. She can detach her ears and use them as mini-boomerangs. You'll like her."

Laughing, I said I was sure I would, then followed Evra and Shancus after the others, to dinner.

It was wonderful to be back with the Cirque Du Freak. I'd been edgy and moody for the last week and a half, thinking about what Evanna had said, but my fears faded within an hour of returning to the circus fold. I met many old friends — Hans Hands, Rhamus Twobellies, Sive and Seersa, Cormac Limbs and Gertha Teeth. I also saw the Wolf Man, but he wasn't quite as welcome a sight as the others, and I kept clear of him as much as possible.

Truska — who could grow a beard at will, then suck the hairs back inside her face — was there too, and delighted to see me. She greeted me in broken English. She hadn't been able to speak the language six years ago, but Evra had been teaching her and she was making good progress. "It is hard," she said as we mingled with the others in a large, run-down school which was serving as the Cirque's base. "I not good at language. But Evra is patient and I slowly learning. I make mistakes still, but—"

"We all make mistakes, gorgeous," Vancha interrupted, popping up beside us. "And yours was not making an honest vampire of me when you had the chance!" He wrapped his arms around Truska and kissed her. She laughed when he let go and waved a finger at him.

"Naughty!" she giggled.

"You two know each other, I take it," I commented dryly.

"Oh, yes," Vancha leered. "We're old friends. Many's the night we went skinny-dipping together in oceans deep and blue, eh, Truska?"

"Vancha," she tutted. "You promised not of that to mention!"

"So I did," he chuckled, then began talking with her in her native tongue. They sounded like a pair of seals barking at each other.

Evra introduced me to Merla, who was very pleasant and pretty. He made her show me her detachable ears. I agreed that they were fabulous, but I declined her offer to let me have a go throwing them.

Mr Crepsley was as pleased to be back as I was. As a dutiful vampire, he'd devoted most of his life to the Generals and their cause, but I suspect his heart lay secretly with the

Cirque Du Freak. He loved to perform and I think he missed being on the stage. Many people asked him if he was back to stay, and expressed disappointment when he said he wasn't. He made light of it, but I think he was genuinely touched by their interest and would have stayed if he could.

There were Little People with the Cirque Du Freak, as usual, but Harkat kept away from them. I tried getting him involved in conversation with others, but people felt nervous around him — they weren't accustomed to a Little Person who could talk. He spent most of the night alone, or in a corner with Shancus, who was fascinated by him and kept asking impolite questions (most to do with whether he was a man or a woman — in fact, like all the Little People, he was neither).

Evanna was known by many people at the Cirque Du Freak, although very few of them had met her before — their parents, grandparents or great-grandparents had told them about her. She spent a few hours mingling and catching up on the past – she had an impressive memory for names and faces – then said her farewells for the night and departed with Mr Tall, to discuss matters strange, portentous and arcane (or else to chat about frogs and magic tricks!).

We retired with the coming of the dawn. We bid goodnight to those still awake, then Evra guided us to our tents. Mr Tall had kept Mr Crepsley's coffin ready for him and the vampire climbed into it with a look of sheer contentment — vampires love their coffins in a way no human can ever understand.

Harkat and me strung up a couple of hammocks and slept in a tent next to Evra and Merla's. Evanna moved into a van adjoining Mr Tall's. And Vancha... Well, when we met him that evening, he swore blind he'd stayed with Truska, and bragged about what a hit he was with the ladies. But by all the leaves and grass stuck to his hair and animal hides, I think it more likely he passed the day by himself under a bush!

CHAPTER SEVENTEEN

HARKAT AND me got up an hour or so before sunset and walked around the camp with Evra and Shancus. I was chuffed that Evra had named his first-born after me and promised to send the boy birthday presents in future, if I could. He wanted me to give him a spider — Evra had told him all about Madam Octa — but I had no intention of sending him one of the poisonous arachnids from Vampire Mountain — I knew from painful experience the trouble a tarantula could cause!

The Cirque Du Freak was much the same as ever. A few new acts had joined, and one or two had parted company with the show, but mostly it was as it had been. Though the circus hadn't changed, *I* had. I sensed that after a while, as we strolled from one caravan or tent to another, pausing to chat with the performers and stagehands. When I lived at the Cirque, I was young — in appearance at least — and people treated me as a child. They didn't any more. While I didn't look that much older, there must have been something different about me, because they no longer spoke down to me.

Although I'd been acting as an adult for years, this was the first time I really thought about how much I'd changed and how I could never return to the lighter days of my youth. Mr Crepsley had been telling me for ages — usually when I complained about how slowly I was maturing — that a night would come when I'd wish I could be young again. Now I realized he was right. My childhood had been a long, drawn-out affair, but within a year or two the purge would rid me of both my human blood and youth, and after that there could be no going back.

"You look pensive," Evra noted.

"I'm thinking about how much things have changed," I sighed. "You married and with kids. Me with worries of my own. Life used to be much simpler."

"It always is for the young," Evra agreed. "I keep telling Shancus that, but he doesn't believe me, any more than we did when we were growing up."

"We're getting old, Evra."

"No we aren't," he said. "We're getting *older*. It'll be decades before I hit old age — centuries for you."

That was true, but I couldn't shake the feeling that I'd somehow grown ancient overnight. For more than twenty-five years I'd lived and thought as a child — Darren Shan, the boy Prince! — but now I didn't feel I was a child any longer.

Mr Crepsley tracked us down as we were devouring hot sausages around a camp fire. Truska had cooked them and was handing them out. The vampire took one, thanked her, and swallowed it in two quick bites. "Savoury," he said, licking his lips, then turned to me with a gleam in his eye. "Would you care to take to the stage tonight? Hibernius has said we may perform."

"What would we do?" I asked. "We don't have Madam Octa any longer."

"I can perform magic tricks, as I did when I first joined the Cirque Du Freak, and you can be my assistant. With our vampiric speed and strength, we can pull off some truly remarkable conjuring feats."

"I dunno," I said. "It's been a long time. I might get stage fright."

"Nonsense. You are doing it. I will not take no for an answer."

"If you put it that way…" I grinned.

"You will need some grooming if we are to present ourselves to the public," Mr Crepsley said, eyeing me critically. "A haircut and manicure are in order."

"I take care of that," Truska said. "I also am having Darren's old pirate costume. I could fix up it to fit him again."

"You've still got that old thing?" I asked, remembering how cool I'd felt when Truska kitted me out as a pirate not long after I'd joined the Cirque Du Freak. I had to leave the fancy clothes behind when I left to travel to Vampire Mountain.

"I am a good holder-on to things," she smiled. "I fetch it and measure you. The suit might not be ready this tonight, but tomorrow I have it in shape. Come to me an hour now from, for measuring."

Vancha was jealous when he heard we were going to be performing. "What about me?" he grumbled. "I know a bit of magic. Why can't I go on too?"

Mr Crepsley stared at the green-haired Prince, with his bare feet, muddy legs and arms, his animal hides and shurikens. He sniffed the air – Vancha had showered in rainfall about six nights earlier, but hadn't washed since – and crinkled his nose. "You are not the essence of presentability, Sire," he remarked carefully.

"What's wrong with me?" Vancha asked, looking down, seeing nothing amiss.

"One must be elegant when one takes to the stage," Mr Crepsley said. "You lack a certain *je ne sais quoi*."

"I don't know about that," I said. "I think there's a perfect part for him in the show."

"There!" Vancha beamed. "The boy has a keen eye."

"He could go on at the start, with the Wolf Man," I said, only barely managing to keep a straight face. "We could pretend they were brothers."

Vancha glared at me as Mr Crepsley, Harkat, Evra and Shancus fell apart with laughter. "You're getting too smart by far!" he snapped, then stormed off to find someone to rant at.

At the appointed time I went to be measured and get my hair cut by Truska. Evra and Shancus also went to prepare for the show, while Harkat helped Mr Crepsley search for props to use in his act.

"Is life being good to you?" Truska asked, snipping my newly-grown fringe.

"It could be worse," I said.

"Vancha told me you now are being a Prince."

"He wasn't supposed to tell anyone," I complained.

"Do not fear. I keep news myself to. Vancha and me old friends. He knows I can a secret keep." She lowered the pair of scissors and looked at me oddly. "Have you seen anything of Mr Tiny since leaving?" she asked.

"That's a strange question," I replied warily.

"He here was, many months ago. Came see Hibernius."

"Oh?" That must have been before his trip to Vampire Mountain.

"Hibernius was troubled after visit. He told me dark times are out in front of us. He said I might be wanting to think of going home to my people. Said I might be safer there."

"Did he say anything about—" I lowered my voice "—the Lord of the Vampaneze or a Master of Shadows?"

She shook her head. "He said only that we was all in for rough nights, and that there much fighting and dying would be before it became over." Then she started clipping again, and after that she measured me for the suit.

I was thinking hard about our conversation when I left Truska's van and went in search of Mr Crepsley. It might be that, prompted by my concerns, my feet led me on purpose to Mr Tall's van, or maybe it was accidental. Either way, I found myself hovering outside a few minutes later, pondering the situation and whether I should ask him about it.

As I stood, deliberating, the door opened and Mr Tall and Evanna emerged. The witch was clad in a black cloak, almost invisible in the darkness of the cloudy night.

"I wish you would not do this," Mr Tall said. "The vampires have been good friends to us. We should help them."

"We cannot take sides, Hibernius," Evanna replied. "It is not our place to decide the twists of fate."

"Still," he muttered, his long face creased, "to embrace these others and parlay with them ... I don't like it."

"We must remain neutral," she insisted. "We have neither allies nor foes among the creatures of the night. If you or I took sides, we could destroy everything. As far as we're concerned, both must be equal, neither good nor bad."

"You are correct," he sighed. "I have spent too long with Larten. I'm letting my friendship for him cloud my judgement."

"There's nothing wrong with befriending these beings," Evanna said. "But we must not get personally involved, not until the future unravels and we have to."

With that, she kissed Mr Tall on the cheek – I don't know how one so short reached all the way up to one so tall, but she did – and slipped away out of camp. Mr Tall watched her go, an unhappy look on his face, then closed the door and went about his business.

I remained where I was a moment, replaying the strange conversation. I wasn't entirely sure what was going on, but I gathered that Evanna was about to do something which Mr Tall didn't like — something that seemed to bode ill for vampires.

As a Prince, I should have waited for Evanna to come back and challenged her openly about the conversation. It wasn't proper for one of my standing to eavesdrop, and it would be positively rude to sneak out of camp after her. But politeness and good manners had never been high on my list of priorities. I'd rather have Evanna think less of me – even punish me for my insolence – and know what she was up to, than let her slip away and face a nasty surprise further down the line.

Kicking off my shoes, I hurried out of camp, spotted the top of her hooded head vanishing behind a tree in the distance – she was moving fast – and set off after her as quickly and quietly as I could.

It was hard keeping up with Evanna. She was swift and sure-footed, leaving almost no trace of her passage. If the chase had endured, I'd have lost her, but she drew to a halt after three or four kilometres, stood breathing in the air a moment, then walked to a small copse of trees, whistled loudly, and entered.

I waited a few minutes to see if she'd emerge. When she didn't, I followed her to the edge of the copse and stood listening. When I heard nothing I slipped between the trees and advanced cautiously. The ground was damp and masked the sounds of my footsteps, but I took no chances: Evanna's sense of hearing was at least as sharp as a vampire's — one snapped twig would be enough to alert her to my presence.

As I progressed, the sound of soft talking reached me. There were several people up ahead, but they were speaking in hushed tones and I was too far away to hear what they were saying. With an increasing sense of unease I crept forward, and finally I was near enough to identify a group of shadowy figures at the heart of the copse.

I didn't move any closer, for fear I'd give myself away, but squatted, watched and listened. Their voices were muffled and only the occasional disconnected word or half-sentence came across. Their voices rose from time to time when they laughed, but even then they were careful not to laugh too loud.

My eyes gradually adjusted to the darkness and I was able to make some sense of the shapes. Apart from Evanna — whose shadow was impossible to mistake — I counted eight people, sitting, squatting or lying down. Seven were large and muscular. The eighth was slight, dressed in a hood and robes, serving drinks and food to the others. They all appeared to be men.

I could be no more certain than that, given the distance and darkness. Either I'd have to get a lot closer to learn more about them, or the moon would have to shine. Glancing up at the cloudy sky through the dense branches of the trees, I figured there wasn't much chance of that. Rising silently, I started to back away.

That's when the servant in the robes lit a candle.

"Put that out, fool!" one of the others barked, and a strong hand knocked the candle to the floor, where a foot roughly quenched it.

"Sorry," the servant squeaked. "I thought we were safe with Lady Evanna."

"We're never safe," the burly man snapped. "Remember that, and don't make such a mistake again."

The men fell back into conversation with Evanna, their voices low and impenetrable, but I was no longer interested in what they had to say. During the few seconds of candlelight, I'd glimpsed purple skin, red eyes and hair, and knew who and what the men were, and why Evanna had been so secretive — she'd come to meet with a group of *vampaneze!*

CHAPTER EIGHTEEN

RETREATING STEALTHILY, I cleared the copse. Seeing no guards, I rushed back to the Cirque Du Freak, pausing neither for breath nor thought. I reached the campsite ten minutes later, having raced as fast as my powers allowed.

The show had commenced and Mr Crepsley was standing in what used to be the church's vestry, watching Rhamus Twobellies eat a tyre. He looked very dashing in his red suit, and he'd rubbed blood along the scar down the left side of his face, drawing attention to it, making him look more mysterious than usual.

"Where have you been?" he snapped as I entered, panting. "I have looked all over for you. I thought I would have to perform alone. Truska has your pirate costume ready. If we hurry, we can—"

"Where's Vancha?" I gasped.

"Off sulking somewhere," Mr Crepsley chuckled. "He

still has not—"

"Larten," I interrupted. He stopped, alerted to the danger by my rare use of his first name. "Forget the show. We have to find Vancha. *Now!*"

He asked no questions. Telling a stagehand to inform Mr Tall of his withdrawal from the bill, he led me out to search for Vancha. We found him with Harkat in the tent I was sharing with the Little Person. He was teaching Harkat how to throw shurikens. Harkat was finding it difficult — his fingers were too large to easily grasp the small stars.

"Look who it is," Vancha jeered as we entered. "The king of the clowns and his head assistant. How's show business, boys?"

I pulled the flap of the tent closed and sunk to my haunches. Vancha saw the serious expression in my eyes and put his shurikens away. Quickly and calmly, I told them what had happened. There was a pause when I finished, broken by Vancha, who let fly with a barbed stream of curses.

"We shouldn't have trusted her," he snarled. "Witches are treacherous by nature. She's probably selling us out to the vampaneze even as we speak."

"I doubt that," Mr Crepsley said. "Evanna would hardly require the aid of the vampaneze if she meant to do us harm."

"You think she's gone over there to discuss frogs?" Vancha barked.

"I do not know what they are discussing, but I do not believe she is betraying us," Mr Crepsley said stubbornly.

"Maybe we should ask Mr Tall," Harkat suggested. "From what Darren says, he knows what Evanna … is up to. Perhaps he would tell us."

Vancha looked at Mr Crepsley. "He's your friend. Should we try?"

Mr Crepsley shook his head. "If Hibernius knew we were in danger, and was capable of warning or aiding us, he would have."

"Very well," Vancha smiled grimly. "We'll have to take them on ourselves." He stood and checked his supply of shurikens.

"We're going to fight them?" I asked, insides tightening.

"We're hardly going to sit here and wait for them to attack!" Vancha replied. "The element of surprise is vital. While we have it, we must make use of it."

Mr Crepsley looked troubled. "Perhaps they do not mean to attack," he said. "We only arrived last night. They could not have known we were coming. Their being here might have nothing to do with us."

"Nonsense!" Vancha howled. "They're here to kill, and if we don't strike first, they'll be on us before—"

"I'm not so sure," I muttered. "Now that I think about it, they weren't on guard or nervous, as they would have been if they were preparing for a fight."

Vancha cursed some more, then sat down again. "OK. Let's say they aren't after us. Perhaps it's coincidence and they don't know we're here." He leant forward. "But they will when Evanna's finished filling them in!"

"You think she'll tell them about us?" I asked.

"We'd be fools to chance it." He cleared his throat. "In case you've forgotten, we're at war. I've nothing personal against our blood-cousins, but for the time being they're our enemies, and we must show them no mercy. Let's say these vampaneze and their servant have nothing to do with our being here. So what? It's our duty to engage them in battle and cut them down."

"That's murder, not self-defence," Harkat said softly.

"Aye," Vancha agreed. "But would you rather we let them go on to murder some of our own? Our quest to find the Vampaneze Lord takes precedence over all else, but when the chance to cull a few stray vampaneze drops our way, we'd be fools — traitors! — not to seize it."

Mr Crepsley sighed. "And Evanna? What if she takes the side of the vampaneze against us?"

"Then we fight her too," Vancha sniffed.

"You fancy your chances against her?" Mr Crepsley smiled thinly.

"No. But I know my duty." He stood, and this time there was a certainty to his stance. "I'm going to kill vampaneze. If you want to come, you can. If not..." He shrugged.

Mr Crepsley looked at me. "What do you say, Darren?"

"Vancha's right," I said slowly. "If we let them go, and they kill vampires later, we'd be to blame. Besides, there's something we're overlooking — the Lord of the Vampaneze." Mr Crepsley and Vancha stared at me. "We're destined to cross paths with him, but I think we have to chase that destiny. Maybe these vampaneze know where he is or will be. I doubt it's coincidence that we're here at the same time as them. This might be fate's way of leading us to him."

"A solid argument," Vancha said.

"Perhaps." Mr Crepsley didn't sound convinced.

"Remember Mr Tiny's words?" I said. "To follow our hearts? My heart says we should face these vampaneze."

"Mine too," Harkat said after a moment's hesitation.

"And mine," Vancha added.

"I thought you had no heart," Mr Crepsley muttered, then stood. "But my heart also demands confrontation, although my head disagrees. We will go."

Vancha grinned bloodthirstily and clapped Mr Crepsley on the back, then without further ado we stole away into the night.

At the copse we made our plans.

"We'll close on them from four different angles," Vancha said, taking charge. "That way we'll make them think there are more of us."

"There are nine of them in all," Mr Crepsley noted, "including Evanna. How do we divide them up?"

"Two vampaneze for you, two for me, two for Harkat. Darren takes the seventh and the servant — he's probably a half-vampaneze or vampet, so he shouldn't pose too much of a problem."

"And Evanna?" Mr Crepsley asked.

"We could all rush her at the end," Vancha suggested.

"No," Mr Crepsley decided. "I will handle her."

"You're sure?"

Mr Crepsley nodded.

"Then all that's left is to split up and move in. Get as close as you can. I'll start by launching a couple of shurikens. I'll aim for arms and legs. Once you hear screams and curses — hit them hard."

"Things would go much smoother if you aimed for throats and heads," I noted.

"I don't fight that way," Vancha growled. "Only cowards kill a foe without facing him. If I have to — as when killing the vampet with the hand grenade — I will, but I prefer to fight cleanly."

The four of us split up and circled the trees, entering the copse at different points. I felt vulnerable and small when I found myself alone in the woods, but quickly thrust such feelings aside and concentrated on my mission. "May the gods of the vampires guide and protect us," I muttered under my breath, before advancing, sword drawn.

The vampaneze and Evanna were still in the clearing at the heart of the copse, talking softly. The moon had broken through the clouds, and although the overhanging branches kept most of the light out, the area was brighter than it had been when I was here before.

Easing forward, I got as close to the vampaneze as I dared, then pulled up behind a thick trunk and waited. All was silent around me. I'd thought Harkat might alert them to our presence — he couldn't move as quietly as a vampire

– but the Little Person was taking great care and made no sound.

I started to count, silently, inside my head. I was up to ninety-six when there was a sharp whistling hiss to my far left, followed by a startled shriek. Less than a second later, another whistle and another scream. Gripping my sword tight, I swung around the tree and darted forward, roaring wildly.

The vampaneze were quick to react, and were on their feet, weapons in hand, by the time I reached them. Fast as they were, Mr Crepsley and Vancha were faster, and as I locked swords with a tall, muscular vampaneze, from whose left shin stuck a silver shuriken, I saw Mr Crepsley cut open the stomach and chest of one of our opponents, killing him instantly, while Vancha's thumb took out the left eye of another — he dropped to the ground, wailing.

I had just enough time to note that the man on the ground wasn't purple-skinned like the rest – a vampet! – then I had to concentrate on the vampaneze in front of me. He was at least two heads taller then me, broader and stronger. But size, as I'd been taught in Vampire Mountain, wasn't everything, and while he lashed out at me with savage strokes, I jabbed and feinted, nicking him here, poking him there, drawing blood, enraging him, spoiling his aim and rhythm, causing him to swing erratically.

As I parried one of his blows, someone stumbled into my back and I tumbled to the ground. Rolling over swiftly, I jumped to my feet and saw a bloody-faced vampaneze fall, gasping for breath. Harkat Mulds stood over him, a red-stained axe in his left hand, an injured right arm hanging limp by his side.

The vampaneze who'd been attacking me now focused on Harkat. With a bellow he swung at the Little Person's head. Harkat brought his axe up just in time, knocked the sword up high of its mark, then stepped back, tempting the vampaneze forward.

I looked around quickly, taking in the state of play. Three of our foes were down, although the vampet who'd lost his eye was scrabbling about for a sword and looked ready to rejoin the action. Mr Crepsley was battling a vampaneze who favoured knives, and the two were swinging around and slicing at each other like a pair of whirling dancers. Vancha had his hands full with a huge, axe-wielding brute. His axe was twice the size of Harkat's, yet he rolled it about between his immense fingers as if it weighed nothing. Vancha was sweating, and bleeding from a cut to his waist, but he wasn't conceding any ground.

Across from me, the seventh vampaneze – tall, slim, with a smooth face, long hair tied back, dressed in a light green suit – and the hooded servant were watching the fighting. Both clutched long swords and stood ready to flee if the battle seemed lost, or dive in and finish things off if they sensed victory. Such cynical tactics disgusted me, and drawing a knife, I sent it whizzing at the head of the servant, who wasn't much bigger than me.

The small man in the robes saw the knife and twitched his head out of the path of its flight. By his swiftness, I knew he must be a blooded creature of the night — no human could have moved so quickly.

The vampaneze next to the servant scowled as I drew another knife, paused a moment, then darted across the clearing before I could take aim. Dropping the knife, I raised my sword and turned his blow aside, but only barely managed to get it up in time to deflect his second strike. He was fast and well-trained in the ways of war. I was in trouble.

I backed away from the vampaneze, protecting myself as best I could. The tip of his sword became a blur as it struck, and though I defended myself ably, his blade soon bit. I felt a wound open on the top of my left arm ... a deep gash to my right thigh ... a jagged scratch across my chest.

I backed up against a tree and caught the sleeve of my right arm on a branch. The vampaneze thrust his sword at my face. I thought the end had come, but then my arm tore free and my sword came across to block his and drive it towards the ground. I pushed down with my sword, hoping to make my foe drop his weapon, but he was too strong and brought his sword up in a smooth reverse movement. His blade slid up the length of mine, giving birth to a shower of sparks. It was moving so fast, and there was so much force behind it, that instead of being routed away by the hilt of my sword when it got there, it cut clean through the gold casing — and clean through the flesh and bone of my sticking-out right thumb!

I screamed as my thumb shot away into the darkness. My sword dropped from my fingers and I fell, defenceless. The vampaneze glanced around casually, dismissing me as a threat. Mr Crepsley was winning the war of the knives — his opponent's face had been slashed to ribbons. Harkat had defied the handicap of his injured arm and buried the tip of his axe deep in his vampaneze's stomach — though the vampaneze bellowed valiantly and fought on, he was surely lost. Vancha was struggling with his opponent, but was holding his own, and when Mr Crepsley or Harkat came to his aid, their combined force would be enough to make an end of the giant. The vampet who'd lost an eye was on his feet, sword in hand, but was swaying unsteadily and wouldn't pose much of a problem.

While all this was happening, Evanna had remained seated on the ground, a neutral look on her face, taking no part in the fighting.

We were going to win and the vampaneze in the green suit knew it. Snarling, he swung once more at my head – aiming to cut it clean off at the neck – but I rolled out of his way, into a pile of leaves. Rather than duck after me to finish me off, he about-faced, ran to where the robed servant was standing, grabbed a spare sword from the ground, then hurried through the trees, pushing the servant ahead of him.

Getting to my feet, I moaned loudly from the pain, then gritted my teeth against it, picked up the knife I'd dropped earlier, and moved in to help Harkat finish off his vampaneze. It wasn't noble, sticking a knife into a warrior's back, but all I cared about was ending the battle, and I felt no pity for the vampaneze when he stiffened and collapsed, my blade buried deep between his shoulder blades.

Mr Crepsley had dispatched the vampaneze with the knives, and after taking care of the one-eyed vampet – a swift cut to his throat – he started forward to help Vancha. That's when Evanna stood and called to him. "Will you raise your blades to *me* too, Larten?"

Mr Crepsley hesitated, knives hovering in his hands, then dropped his guard and went on one knee before her. "Nay, Lady," he sighed. "I will not."

"Then I will not raise a hand to you," she said, and commenced walking from one dead vampaneze to another, kneeling beside them, making the death's touch, whispering, "Even in death may you be triumphant."

Mr Crepsley got to his feet and studied Vancha as he battled the largest of the vampaneze. "A close call, Sire," he noted dryly as the giant barely missed the top of Vancha's scalp with his huge war axe. Vancha honoured Mr Crepsley with one of his foulest curses in reply. "Would you be offended if I offered my assistance, Sire?" Mr Crepsley asked politely.

"Get over here quick!" Vancha snarled. "Two are getting away. We have to— *Charna's guts!*" he yelled, again only barely dodging the head of the axe.

"Harkat, stay with me," Mr Crepsley said, moving forward to intercept the giant. "Darren, go with Vancha after the others."

"Right," I said. I didn't mention the fact that I was missing a thumb — such considerations were nothing in the heat of life or death battle.

As Mr Crepsley and Harkat engaged the giant, Vancha swung away, paused for breath, then nodded for me to follow as he raced after the vampaneze and the servant. I kept close to him, sucking on the bloody stump where my thumb used to be, grabbing a knife from my belt with my left hand. As we broke from the trees, we saw the pair ahead. The servant was climbing on to the vampaneze's back — it was clear that they were planning to flit.

"No you don't!" Vancha growled, and sent a dark shuriken flying. It struck the servant high above the right shoulder blade. He cried out and toppled off the vampaneze's back. The vampaneze spun, stooped to pick up his fallen comrade, saw Vancha closing in, and jumped to his feet, pulling a sword and moving forward. I hung back, not wanting to get in Vancha's way, keeping an eye on the fallen servant, waiting to see how the fight progressed.

Vancha was almost within striking distance of the vampaneze when he drew up short, as though injured. I thought he must have been hit with something – a knife or arrow – but he didn't look hurt. He just stood, arms outstretched, staring at the vampaneze. The vampaneze was motionless too, his red eyes wide, his dark purple face incredulous. Then he lowered his sword, slid it into its scabbard, turned and picked up the servant.

Vancha did nothing to stop him.

Behind me I heard Mr Crepsley and Harkat break free of the trees. They raced forward, then stopped by my side when they saw the vampaneze escaping, Vancha standing by and watching.

"What the—" Mr Crepsley began, but then the vampaneze hit flitting speed and disappeared.

Vancha looked back at us, then sank to the ground. Mr Crepsley cursed — not quite as foul as Vancha's earlier outburst, but close — and sheathed his knives in disgust. "You let them escape!" he shouted. Striding forward, he stood over Vancha and regarded him with undisguised contempt. "*Why?*" he growled, hands bunched into fists.

"I couldn't stop him," Vancha whispered, eyes downcast.

"You did not even try!" Mr Crepsley roared.

"I couldn't fight him," Vancha said. "I always feared this night would come. I prayed it wouldn't, but part of me knew it would."

"You are not making sense!" Mr Crepsley snapped. "Who was that vampaneze? Why did you let him escape?"

"His name is Gannen Harst," Vancha said in a low, broken voice. He looked up and there were hard, glittering tears in his eyes. "He's my *brother*."

CHAPTER NINETEEN

FOR A long time nothing was said. Harkat, Mr Crepsley and me stared at Vancha, whose eyes were fixed on the ground. Overhead the moon had vanished behind thick banks of cloud. When they finally parted, Vancha began to talk, as though prompted by the moonbeams.

"My real name's Vancha Harst," he said. "I changed it when I became a vampire. Gannen's a year or two younger than me — or is it the other way round? It's been so long, I can't remember. We were very close growing up. We did everything together — including joining the vampaneze.

"The vampaneze who blooded us was an honest man and a good teacher. He told us exactly what our lives would be like. He explained their ways and beliefs, how they looked upon themselves as the guardians of history by keeping alive the memories of those they drank from." (If a vampire or vampaneze drains a person's blood, he absorbs part of their spirit and memories.) "He said vampaneze killed when they drank, but did it swiftly and painlessly."

"That makes it OK?" I snorted.

"To the vampaneze, yes," Vancha said.

"How can you—" I started to explode.

Mr Crepsley stopped me with a soft wave of his hand. "This is not the time for a moral debate. Let Vancha talk."

"There's not a whole lot more to tell," Vancha said. "Gannen and I were blooded as half-vampaneze. We served together for a few years as assistants. I couldn't accustom myself to the killing. So I quit."

"As simply as that?" Mr Crepsley asked sceptically.

"No," Vancha said. "The vampaneze normally don't permit assistants to live if they choose to part company with the clan. No vampaneze will kill one of his own, but that law doesn't apply to a half-vampaneze. My master should have killed me when I said I wanted out.

"Gannen saved me. He pleaded for my life. When that failed, he said our master would have to kill him also. In the end my life was spared, but I was warned to avoid all vampaneze in future, including Gannen, whom I never saw again until tonight.

"For several years I lived miserably. I tried feeding as vampires do, not killing those I fed upon, but vampaneze blood exerts a powerful hold. I'd lose control when I fed, and kill in spite of myself. In the end I made up my mind not to feed at all, and die. It was then that I met Paris Skyle, who took me under his wing."

"Paris blooded you?" Mr Crepsley asked.

"Yes."

"Even though he knew what you were?"

Vancha nodded.

"But how can you blood someone as a vampire if he's already been blooded as a vampaneze?" I asked.

"It is possible for those who are not fully blooded," Mr Crepsley said. "A half-vampire can become a vampaneze, and vice versa, but it is dangerous and rarely attempted. I know of only three other cases — and twice it ended in death, for both the blooder and the blooded."

"Paris knew the risks," Vancha said, "but didn't tell me about them until afterwards. I wouldn't have gone through with it if I'd known his life was in danger."

"What did he have to do?" Harkat asked.

"Take my blood and give me his, the same as any ordinary blooding," Vancha said. "The only difference was, half my blood was vampaneze, which is poisonous to vampires. Paris took my tainted blood, and his body's natural defences broke it down and rendered it harmless. But it could have easily killed him, just as his blood could have killed me. But the luck of the vampires was with us — we both survived, though our agonies were great.

"With my vampaneze blood transformed by Paris's blood, I was able to control my feeding urges. I studied under Paris and in time trained to be a General. My vampaneze links were revealed to no one except the other Princes."

"They approved of your blooding?" Mr Crepsley asked.

"After I'd proven myself many times — yes. They worried about Gannen — they were afraid my loyalties would be divided if I met him again, as they have been tonight — but they accepted me and vowed to keep my true history a secret."

"Why wasn't *I* told about you?" I asked.

"Had I come to Vampire Mountain while you were there, you would have been told. But it's impolite to speak of one when he's absent."

"This is damned frustrating," Mr Crepsley grunted. "I understand why you did not speak of it before, but if we had known, *I* could have gone after your brother and left you to take care of that giant in the trees."

"How was I to know?" Vancha smiled weakly. "I didn't see his face until I was moving in for the kill. He was the last person I expected to run into."

Behind us, Evanna emerged from between the trees. Her hands were red with the blood of dead vampaneze. She was carrying something. As she got closer, I realized it was my missing thumb. "Found this," she said, tossing it to me. "Thought you might like it back."

I caught the thumb, then looked down at the stump where it had been cut off. I hadn't been aware of the pain while listening to Vancha talk, but now the throbbing intensified. "Can we stitch it back on?" I winced.

"Possibly," Mr Crepsley said, examining the stump and thumb. "Lady Evanna — you have the power to connect it immediately and effortlessly, do you not?"

165

"I do," Evanna agreed, "but I won't. Snoops don't deserve special favours." She wagged a finger at me. "You should have been a spy, Darren." It was hard to tell whether she was annoyed or amused.

Vancha had string and a needle made from fish bone, and while Mr Crepsley held my thumb in place, the Prince stitched it back on, even though his thoughts were elsewhere. It hurt tremendously, but I just had to look away and grit my teeth. The stitching completed, the vampires rubbed their spit around the join, to quicken the healing process, strapped the thumb tight to my fingers so that the bones could fuse, then let me be.

"That is the best we can do," Mr Crepsley said. "If it gets infected, we will chop it off again and you will have to make do without."

"That's right," I growled. "Look on the bright side."

"It's my head you should be chopping off," Vancha said bitterly. "I should have put duty before kinship. I don't deserve to live."

"Nonsense!" Mr Crepsley huffed. "Any man who would strike a brother is no man at all. You did what any of us would have done. It is unfortunate that you ran into him now, but we have not been harmed by your slip, and I think—"

He stopped at a sudden burst of laughter from Evanna. The witch was giggling wildly, as if he'd cracked a great joke.

"Did I say something funny?" Mr Crepsley asked, bemused.

"Oh, Larten, if only you knew!" she squealed.

He raised an eyebrow at Vancha, Harkat and me. "What is she laughing at?"

None of us knew.

"Never mind why she's laughing," Vancha said, stepping forward to confront the witch. "*I* want to know what she was doing here in the first place, and why she was consorting with the enemy while pretending to be our ally."

Evanna stopped laughing and faced Vancha. She grew magically, until she was towering over him like a coiled cobra, but the Prince didn't flinch. Gradually the menace drained out of her and she resorted to her standard shape. "I never claimed to be your ally, Vancha," she said. "I travelled with you, and broke bread with you — but I never said I was on your side."

"Does that mean you're on *theirs?*" he snarled.

"I take nobody's side," she replied coolly. "The divide between vampires and vampaneze is of no interest to me. I look upon you as silly, warring boys, who will one night come to their senses and stop spitting angrily at one another."

"An interesting view," Mr Crepsley remarked ironically.

"I don't understand," I said. "If you aren't on their side, what were you doing with them?"

"Conversing," she said. "Taking their measure, as I did with you. I've sat with the hunters and studied them. Now I've done likewise with the hunted. Whichever way the War of the Scars goes, I'll have to deal with the victors. It's good to know in advance the calibre of those to whom your future is tied."

"Can anyone make sense of this?" Vancha asked.

Evanna smirked, delighted by our confusion. "Do you fine, fighting gentlemen read mystery novels?" she asked. We stared at her blankly. "If you did, you'd have guessed by now what's going on."

"Have you ever hit a woman?" Vancha asked Mr Crepsley.

"No," he said.

"*I* have," Vancha grunted.

"Temper," the witch giggled, then grew serious. "If you have something that is precious, and others are looking for it, where is the best place to hide it?"

"If this rubbish continues..." Vancha warned.

"It's not rubbish," Evanna said. "Even humans know the answer to this one."

We thought about it in silence. Then I raised a hand, as though in school, and said, "Out in the open, in front of everyone?"

"Exactly," Evanna applauded. "People searching — or hunting — rarely find what they seek if it's placed directly before them. It's common to overlook that which is most obvious."

"What does any of this have to do with—" Mr Crepsley began.

"The man in the robes ... was no servant," Harkat interrupted grimly. Our heads turned questioningly. "That's what we overlooked ... wasn't it?"

"Precisely," the witch said, and now there was a touch of sympathy to her tone. "By dressing and treating him as a servant — as they have since they took to the road — the vampaneze knew he'd be the last target anyone would focus on in the event of an attack." Holding up four fingers, Evanna slowly bent the index one over, and said, "Your brother didn't run because he was afraid, Vancha. He fled to save the life of the man he was protecting — the fake servant — the *Lord of the Vampaneze!*"

CHAPTER TWENTY

UNDER ORDERS from Evanna — she threatened to blind and deafen us if we disobeyed — we buried the dead vampaneze and vampet in the copse, digging deep graves and placing them on their backs, facing towards the sky and Paradise, before covering them over.

Vancha was inconsolable. On our return to the Cirque Du Freak, he demanded a bottle of brandy, then locked himself away in a small trailer and refused to answer our calls. He blamed himself for the escape of the Vampaneze Lord. If he'd tackled his brother, the Vampaneze Lord would have been at our mercy. It was the first of our four promised chances to kill him, and it was hard to imagine a simpler opportunity falling into our laps.

Mr Tall already knew what had happened. He'd been expecting the confrontation and told us that the vampaneze had been trailing the Cirque Du Freak for more than a month.

"They knew we were coming?" I asked.

"No," he said. "They were following us for other reasons."

"But *you* knew we were coming ... didn't you?" Harkat challenged him.

Mr Tall nodded sadly. "I'd have warned you, but the consequences would have been dire. Those with insight into the future are forbidden to influence it. Only Desmond Tiny can meddle directly in the affairs of time."

"Do you know where they have gone," Mr Crepsley asked, "or when we are due to clash with them again?"

"No," Mr Tall said. "I could find out, but I read the future as little as possible. What I *can* tell you is that Gannen Harst is prime protector of the Lord of the Vampaneze. The six you killed were normal guards who can be replaced. Harst is the key guardian. Where the Lord goes, he goes too. Had he been killed, the odds of future success would have weighed heavily on your side."

"If only I had gone after Harst instead of Vancha," Mr Crepsley sighed.

Evanna, who'd said nothing since we returned, shook her head. "Don't waste time regretting lost chances," she said. "You weren't destined to face Gannen Harst at this stage of the hunt. Vancha was. It was fate."

"Let's be positive," I said. "We now know who the Vampaneze Lord is travelling with. We can spread Gannen Harst's description and tell our people to look out for him. And they won't be able to pull that servant disguise again — next time we'll be ready and know who to look for."

"This is true," Mr Crepsley agreed. "Plus we have suffered no losses. We are as strong as we were at the start of our quest, we are wiser, and we still have three chances to kill him."

"Then why do we feel ... so terrible?" Harkat asked glumly.

"Failure is always a bitter pill to swallow," Mr Crepsley said.

We saw to our wounds after that. Harkat's arm was badly cut but no bones were broken. We set it in a sling, and Mr Crepsley said it would be fine in a couple of nights. My right thumb was turning an ugly colour, but Mr Tall said it wasn't infected and would be OK if I rested it.

We were preparing for sleep when we heard angry bellows. Hurrying through the camp – Mr Crepsley with a heavy cloak tossed over his head to protect him from the morning sun – we found Vancha on the outskirts, tearing off his clothes, an empty bottle of brandy on the ground beside him, screaming at the sun. "Roast me!" he challenged it. "I don't care! Do your worst! See if I give a–"

"Vancha!" Mr Crepsley snapped. "What are you doing?"

Vancha whirled, snatched up the bottle and pointed it at Mr Crepsley as though it was a knife. "Stay away!" he hissed. "I'll kill you if you try to stop me!"

Mr Crepsley came to a halt. He knew better than to mess with a drunken vampire, especially one of Vancha's powers. "This is stupid, Sire," he said. "Come inside. We will find another bottle of brandy and help you drink–"

"—to the health of the Vampaneze Lord!" Vancha shrieked crazily.

"Sire, this is madness," Mr Crepsley said.

"Aye," Vancha agreed in a sadder, sober tone. "But this is a mad world, Larten. Because I spared the life of my brother — who once saved mine — our greatest enemy has escaped and our people face defeat. What sort of a world is it where evil is born of an act of goodness?"

Mr Crepsley had no answer for that.

"Dying will not help, Vancha," Harkat said. "*I* should know."

"It won't help," Vancha agreed, "but it will punish, and I deserve to be punished. How could I face my fellow Princes and Generals after this? My chance to kill the Lord of the Vampaneze has passed. Better I pass with it than linger and shame us all."

"So you plan on staying out here and letting the sun kill you?" I asked.

"Aye," he chuckled.

"You're a coward," I sneered.

His expression hardened. "Take heed, Darren Shan — I'm in the mood to crack a few skulls before I die!"

"And a fool," I pressed on, regardless. I stormed past Mr Crepsley and pointed accusingly at Vancha with my good left hand. "Who gave you the right to quit? What makes you think you can abandon the quest and damn us all?"

"What are you talking about?" he stammered, confused. "I'm no longer part of the quest. It's up to you and Larten now."

"Is it?" Turning, I searched for Evanna and Mr Tall. I found them together, behind the crowd of circus performers and assistants which had been attracted by the howls of the Prince. "Lady Evanna. Mr Tall. Answer if you may — does Vancha still have a part to play in the hunt for the Vampaneze Lord?"

Mr Tall shared an uneasy glance with Evanna. She hesitated, then said grudgingly, "He has the power to influence the quest."

"But I failed," Vancha said, bewildered.

"*Once,*" I agreed. "But who's to say you won't have another chance? Nobody said we'd have one chance each. For all we know, all four opportunities are destined to fall to *you!*"

Vancha blinked, and his mouth slowly opened.

"Even if the chances are to be shared evenly," Mr Crepsley chipped in, "there are a further three to go, and Darren and I are only two — therefore one of us must be destined to face the Vampaneze Lord twice if it goes down to the final encounter."

Vancha wavered on his feet, considering our words, then dropped the bottle and stumbled towards me. I caught and steadied him. "I've been an idiot, haven't I?" he groaned.

"Yes," I agreed, smiling, then led him back into the shade, where he joined us in slumber until the darkening of night.

We arose with the sinking of the sun and gathered in Mr Tall's van. As dusk deepened, and Vancha drank mug after mug of steaming hot coffee to cure his hangover, we debated our next move and decided it would be for the best if we left the Cirque Du Freak. I would have liked to stay on longer, and so would Mr Crepsley, but our destiny lay elsewhere. Besides, Gannen Harst might return with an army of vampaneze, and we didn't want to find ourselves boxed in, or bring the wrath of our foes down upon the circus folk.

Evanna would not be travelling with us. The witch told us she was returning to her cave and frogs, to prepare for the tragedies to come. "And there *will* be tragedies," she said, a sparkle in her brown and green eyes. "Whether for the vampires or vampaneze, I don't yet know. But it must end in tears for one set, that much is certain."

I can't say I missed the short, hairy, ugly witch when she left — her dark predictions had brought nothing but gloom into our lives, and I thought we were better off without her.

Vancha would also be departing by himself. We'd agreed that he should return to Vampire Mountain and tell the others of our encounter with the Lord of the Vampaneze. They needed to know about Gannen Harst. Vancha would link up with us again later, by tracking Mr Crepsley's mental waves.

We bid short farewells to our friends at the Cirque Du Freak. Evra was sad that I had to leave so soon, but he knew my life was complicated. Shancus was even sadder — it would be his birthday soon and he'd been anticipating a wonderful present. I told the snake-boy I'd find something exciting on the road and send it to him – although I couldn't guarantee it would reach him in time for his birthday — and that cheered him up.

Truska asked if I wanted to take my newly tailored pirate costume with me. I told her to hang on to it — it would only get stained and torn during my travels. I swore I'd be back to try it out. She said I'd better, then treated me to a long goodbye kiss which had Vancha seething with jealousy.

Mr Tall met us at the edge of camp as we were about to leave. "Sorry I couldn't come earlier," he said. "Business to deal with. The show must go on."

"Take care, Hibernius," Mr Crepsley said, shaking the tall man's hand. For once Mr Tall didn't shirk away from the contact.

"You too, Larten," he replied, a grave expression on his face. Looking around at us, he said, "Dark times lie ahead, regardless of the outcome of your quest. I want you to know that there will always be a home for you — *all* of you — here at the Cirque Du Freak. I can't play as active a part in the deciding of the future as I wish, but I *can* offer sanctuary."

We thanked him for his offer, then watched as he walked away and was swallowed by the shadows of his beloved circus camp.

Facing each other, we hesitated, reluctant to part.

"Well!" Vancha boomed eventually. "Time I was off. It's a long trek to Vampire Mountain, even when flitting." Vampires weren't supposed to flit on the way to the mountain fortress, but the rules had been relaxed during wartime to allow for quicker communication between Generals and Princes.

Each of us shook Vancha's hand. I felt miserable at the thought of parting with the red-skinned, sun-fighting Prince. "Cheer up," he laughed at my gloomy expression. "I'll be back in time to lead the second charge against the Vampaneze Lord. You have my word, and Vancha March never broke..." He paused. "'March' or 'Harst'?" he mused aloud, then spat into the dirt at his feet. "Charna's guts! I've gone this long as Vancha March — I'll stick with it."

Saluting, he turned abruptly and jogged away. Soon he was running. Then, in a flash, he hit flitting speed and was lost to sight.

"And then there were three," Mr Crepsley muttered, gazing at Harkat and me.

"Back where we started six years ago," I said.

"But we had a destination then," Harkat noted. "Where are we going ... this time?"

I looked to Mr Crepsley for an answer.

He shrugged. "We can decide later. For now, let us simply walk."

Hoisting our bags on to our backs, we spared the Cirque Du Freak one last, lingering glimpse, then faced the cold, unwelcoming darkness and set forth, surrendering ourselves to the forces of destiny and future terrors of the night.

TO BE CONTINUED...

ALLIES
OF THE NIGHT

SOMETHING STRUCK the back of my head, hard, from behind and I went toppling into the rubbish. I cried out as I fell, then rolled away defensively, clutching the back of my head between my hands. As I rolled, a silver object came crashing down on the ground where my head had been, and sparks flew.

Ignoring my wounded head, I scrambled to my knees and looked for something to defend myself with. The plastic top of a dustbin lay nearby. It wouldn't be much good but it was all I could find. Stooping swiftly, I snatched it up and held it in front of me like a shield, turning to meet the charge of my assailant, who was streaking towards me at a speed no human could have matched.

Something gold flashed and swung down upon my makeshift shield, cutting the dustbin lid in half. Somebody chuckled, and it was the sound of pure, insane evil.

"I'll cut you to pieces!" my attacker boasted, circling me warily. There was something familiar about his voice, but try as I might, I couldn't place it.

I studied his outline as he swung around me. He was wearing dark clothes and his face was masked by a balaclava. The ends of a beard jutted out from underneath it. He was large and chunky and I could see two blood-red eyes glinting above his snarling teeth. He had no hands, just two metallic attachments — one gold, the other silver — at the ends of his arms. There were three hooks on each, sharp, curved, deadly.

The vampaneze – the eyes and speed were the giveaway – struck. He was fast, but I avoided the killer hooks, which dug into the wall behind me and gouged out a sizeable crater when he pulled free. It took less than a second for my attacker to free his hand, but I used that time to strike, kicking him in the chest. But he'd been expecting it and brought his other arm down upon my shin, cruelly knocking my leg aside.

I yelped as pain shot up the length of my leg. Hopping madly, I threw the two halves of the useless dustbin lid at the vampaneze. He ducked out of the way, laughing. I tried to run — no good. My injured leg wouldn't support me, and after a couple of strides I collapsed to the floor, helpless.

I whirled over on to my back and stared up at the hook-handed vampaneze as he took his time approaching. He swung his arms back and forth as he got closer, the hooks making horrible screeching noises as they scraped together. "Going to cut you," the vampaneze hissed. "Slow and painful. I'll start on your fingers. Slice them off, one at a time. Then your hands. Then your toes. Then—"

There was a dull boom, followed by the hiss of parted air. Something shot by the vampaneze's head, only narrowly missing. It struck the wall and stuck — a short, thick, steel-tipped arrow. The vampaneze cursed and crouched, hiding in the shadows of the alley.

Moments ticked by like spiders scuttling up my spine. The vampaneze's angry breath and my gasping sobs filled the air. There was no sight or sound of the person who'd fired the arrow. Shuffling backwards, the vampaneze locked gazes with me and bared his teeth. "I'll get you later," he vowed. "You'll die slowly, in great agony. I'll cut you. Fingers first. One at a time." Then he turned and sprinted. A second arrow was fired after him, but he ducked low and again it missed, burying itself in a large bag of rubbish. The vampaneze exploded out of the end of the alley and vanished quickly into the night.

There was a lengthy pause. Then footsteps. A man of medium height appeared out of the gloom. He was dressed in black, with a long scarf looped around his neck, and gloves covering his hands. He had grey hair – though he wasn't old – and there was a stern set to his features. He was holding a gun-shaped weapon, out of the end of which jutted a steel-tipped arrow. Another of the arrow-firing guns was slung over his left shoulder.

I sat up, grunting, and tried to rub some life back into my right leg. "Thanks," I said as the man got closer. He didn't answer, just proceeded to the end of the alley, where he scanned the area beyond for signs of the vampaneze.

Turning, the grey-haired man came back and stopped a couple of metres away. He was holding the arrow gun in his right hand, but it wasn't pointed harmlessly down at the ground — it was pointing at *me*.

"Mind lowering that?" I asked, forcing a sheepish smile. "You just saved my life. Be a shame if that went off by accident and killed me."

He didn't reply immediately. Nor did he lower the gun. There was no warmth in his expression. "Does it surprise you that I spared your life?" he asked. As with the vampaneze, there was something familiar about this man's voice, but again I couldn't place it.

"I . . . guess," I said weakly, nervously eyeing the arrow-gun.

"Do you know why I saved you?"

I gulped. "Out of the goodness of your heart?"

"Maybe." He took a step closer. The tip of the gun was now aimed directly at my heart. If he fired, he'd create a hole the size of a football in my chest. "Or maybe I was saving you for myself!" he hissed.

DARREN SHAN
CIRQUE DU FREAK

THE SAGA OF DARREN SHAN
BOOK 1

Darren Shan is just an ordinary schoolboy – until he gets an invitation to visit the Cirque Du Freak… until he meets Madam Octa… until he comes face to face with a creature of the night.

Soon, Darren and his friend Steve are caught in a deadly trap. Darren must make a bargain with the one person who can save Steve. But that person is not human and only deals in blood…

ISBN 978 0 00 675416 9

www.darrenshan.com

DARREN SHAN

THE
VAMPIRE'S ASSISTANT

THE SAGA OF DARREN SHAN
BOOK 2

Darren Shan was just an ordinary schoolboy – until
his visit to the Cirque Du Freak. Now, as he
struggles with his new life as a Vampire's Assistant,
he tries desperately to resist the one thing that can
keep him alive… blood. But a gruesome encounter
with the Wolf Man may change all that…

ISBN 978 0 00 675513 5

www.darrenshan.com

DARREN SHAN
TUNNELS OF BLOOD

THE SAGA OF DARREN SHAN
BOOK 3

Darren Shan, the Vampire's Assistant, get's a taste of
city life when he leaves the Cirque Du Freak with
Evra and Mr Crepsley. At night the vampire goes
about secret business, while by day Darren enjoys his
freedom.

But then bodies are discovered... Corpses drained of
blood... The hunt for the killer is on and Darren's
loyalties are tested to the limit as he fears the worst.
One mistake and they are all doomed to perish in the
tunnels of blood...

ISBN 978 0 00 675514 2

www.darrenshan.com

DARREN SHAN
VAMPIRE MOUNTAIN

THE SAGA OF DARREN SHAN
BOOK 4

Darren Shan and Mr Crepsley embark on a dangerous trek to the very heart of the vampire world. But they face morethan the cold on Vampire Mountain – the vampaneeze have been there before them...

Will a meeting with the Vampire Princes restore Darren's human side, or turn him further towards the darkness? Only one thing is certain – Darren's initiation into the vampire clan is more deadly than he can ever have imagined.

ISBN 978 0 00 711441 2

www.darrenshan.com

DARREN SHAN
TRIALS OF DEATH

THE SAGA OF DARREN SHAN
BOOK 5

The Trials: seventeen ways to die unless the luck of the vampires is with you. Darren Shan must pass five fearsome Trials to prove himself to the vampire clan — or face the stakes in the Hall of Death.

But Vampire Mountain holds hidden threats. Sinister, potent forces are gathering in the darkness. In this nightmare world of bloodshed and betrayal, death may be a blessing...

ISBN 978 0 00 711440 5

www.darrenshan.com